the lavender child

harriet richards

the lavender child

harriet richards

THE LAVENDER CHILD
By Harriet Richards

Shadowpaw Press Reprise
Regina, Saskatchewan, Canada
www.shadowpawpress.com

Second edition

First edition published 1997
by Thistledown Press

Cover painting by Harriet Richards

Trade Paperback ISBN: 978-1-998273-20-1
Ebook ISBN: 978-1-998273-21-8

Shadowpaw Press is grateful for
the financial support of Creative Saskatchewan.

For Benjamin

ONE

September

Louise was crouched awkwardly by the little rock garden. She worked slowly and considered each strand of quack grass as she plucked it from the silver mound in a lazy and syrupy way. The afternoon sun wore her into a numbed heaviness. Sweat trickled between breasts and belly. She felt huge.

She unbent a little and shifted toward the dianthus. It had thrived over the summer and sat fussily beside the sandstone, a lady's hat topped in Sunday pink. As she pulled new weeds from its border of earth, she noticed something glint beside her hand. A tiny lamé purse. The twins had been heartless with their handed-down treasures. They used to stage wars, leaving Barbie and GI Joe casualties, dismembered or headless, all over the yard.

Louise brushed particles of dirt from the purse and placed the strap around the smallest finger of her left hand.

It was the sort of discovery Celia might easily have made when she was two, following her mother as she turned the neglected and dry-packed city dirt twice with a long-handled spade. Louise had looked back and found her, plump fingers deft as a monkey's, picking out broken glass and bits of rusted metal and dropping them into her toy pail. Celia unearthed things Louise missed: an iridescent bronze beetle struggling with a cracked wing, a faded inch-high red cowboy, two blackened dimes.

The potatoes she'd grown softened and sprouted that first winter in a warm basement. Most of the newspaper-wrapped green tomatoes ended up in the garbage. She'd spent every spare hour for weeks freezing corn and beets and peas, refusing her mother's offers of canning equipment. She couldn't risk scalding her children.

Five daughters needed a lawn, a paddling pool, and a swing set. The vegetable patch wasn't much by her mother's standards; it shrank into a quilt of the simplest plants—squares of marigold, thyme, alyssum, chives, tiny tims—separated from the fruit trees by a narrow brick path Gavin had laid. The garden changed every year. She grew it for love, finally, the only way it made sense.

Her knees were stiff, and a charley horse began to seize a foot. Louise worked her way upright and waited until the breeze caught under her smock and cooled the dampness of her thighs. *Stupid to be out here this long.* She staggered into the porch and through the kitchen door, kicked off her sandals, and sprawled into their old platform rocker.

The rocker was motionless for the hour as she slept, her breathing deep and rhythmic.

A blue bottle fly wandered in from the dining room and bounced around the room, making angry little cat sounds. *Buzz growl.* Settled on her belly.

A tiny fist punched upward, hard, from under her smock, and the fly rose, spinning, surprised. Louise mumbled something, dreaming about salty seas and the Kraken. The fist retracted. The fly circled for another landing, analyzed strands of black hair, freckled shoulders, then touched down on the same place.

Punch. The Kraken. It drifts heavily, lazily, uncoiling enormous muscled tentacles; the watery beat of its heart echoes along inky eddies.

The fly brushed Louise's upper lip. She frowned in sleep and pushed at her face.

A door opened somewhere.

Footsteps crept into the edge of her dream. Familiar, demanding. The sea had faded, the faintly disquieting figure within retreating as Louise struggled to break the surface of sleep, fighting the bone weariness that consumed her as she approached the end of this pregnancy.

She managed to squint up at the misty form of Celia, whose grin had the effect of bringing Louise to full consciousness.

"Sorry, Mom, it's just me. Close your eyes again. You were such a vision slumped there with your mouth open and dirty feet sticking out."

"Never mind, I'm awake now. Help me up. I'm so tired I could die."

Celia squatted and put her arms around her mother, resting her cheek on the warm swell of her unborn brother. "Hey, Bump, you're pretty rowdy today."

"I was dreaming when you came in, can't remember exactly, something about the Kraken."

Celia stood and began to hoist Louise from the rocker. "The Kraken? What, was one of us lashed to the rocks to tempt the monster? Not like you haven't got enough virgin daughters to keep him happy for a while. Anyhow, I read someplace you're not supposed to think about weird stuff when you're pregnant."

"It didn't feel too sinister. Probably came from Hazel and Fay watching *Clash of the Titans* over and over." Louise resisted making a crack about the virgin prerequisite. She really would rather not know if Celia still qualified, and Louise lacked the energy to tackle any difficult conversations.

Celia's hand caught the little purse on her mother's finger. She peered at it and then shrieked, "There it is! Oh my God, Mom, where did you find it?"

Louise was standing now, unsteadily and pleased, as Celia wiggled the purse off and inspected it affectionately. She held it by the tips of thumb and pointy finger and performed a Barbie kind of walk to the counter. Smiled at it again. "I loved these things." But she tossed her treasure next to the toaster and started to rummage through the fridge.

Her hair fell down her back, long and fine, almost dark enough to be black, but the window's light caught its tinge of auburn. She slammed the fridge door. "Why don't we ever have real food?"

"There's peanut butter. And those bananas are still good. Anybody else home?"

"I don't know where they are. I ran back to eat something; I'm starving. Barely September, and already, Drama's started after school. God, I think I'm going to hate this play; it offends me somebody actually got paid for writing it. The ones we do for competition are lots better." She downed a glass of milk, scrutinized her mother. "You okay? You look pretty wiped out. I really don't think you should wear lilac—you're too pale."

"Is this lilac? I thought the label said 'dove.'"

"Let me take you shopping next time."

"Next time, I won't be buying tents. I hope to slip sveltely into my own clothes."

"That's exactly what I'm afraid of. Let me take you shopping."

"All right." For such a sophisticated girl, her daughter was making short and noisy work of her sandwich.

On the way to the bathroom, Louise turned on the radio, loosing bright violin into the air. She flinched as the load nagged against her bladder, baby limbs reaching and kicking.

"Quit dancing out there, Celia; you're getting the Bump worked up."

The Bump.

She'd had a dream. Eight months ago.

She swam in a hot night sea, floating on black swells streaked with the colour of old red wine, phosphorescence weaving the waves like constellations. A deep, satisfying swim. All alone, she was trying to go somewhere; wanted to finish something. But her eyes opened. Gavin relaxed his weight onto her; his arms were under her head, his breath in her ear. He said, "I dreamed I built a fence; I was hammering." Then he was laughing, and she laughed, Gavin's back bouncing under her arm. But she knew what had happened and could already feel the beginnings of their first son.

Louise was a disaffected Catholic, casual and skeptical, but she prayed for her daughters and had them baptized just the same. Sometimes, friends assumed that the Pope was the indirect cause of her fecundity, and she'd laugh. "Think how many of the little beggars we'd have had if we didn't use birth control." Gavin brewed his own religion, adding things randomly to a bag of beliefs.

This wasn't their only child conceived in a dream—their eldest daughter, Celia, was given her celestial name because of it. But Louise was sure the Bump would be their first boy, and they had already decided to name him Dion. She had complained to Gavin about his dream of building and hammering at the time of conception; now, they would have to buy new clothes and rely less on hand-me-downs.

Louise washed her face. This one was tough. She was always tired. Her iron count was low—although she told her young doctor the anemia would disappear the moment she gave birth, it always did. But she didn't remember this listlessness from the other times. Thirty-eight years old and having another damned baby. She was thankful for the girls—they were so thrilled, and there would be no end of babysitters for him—but she felt like a prize breeding sow. Everything that happened was big news: every prenatal visit to the doctor, every urine test, was the subject of family discussion. The girls played their favourite music to her abdomen, stroked and talked to it, and consulted it like the oracle. "What do you think, Bump? Should I try out for this play?" "Should I cut my hair short?" "What should I do my report on, Bump?"

Louise, the worthy vessel. The Bump was their mystery, alive but invisible, warm and untouchable. The girls would embrace their mother and feel not only her own strength but that of the one she carried, this perfect, quiet human being who had no history, no worries, just uncluttered, pure experience. A blessed person.

When Morgan, at the fragile age of twelve, worried that her strong legs looked fat or was teased about not having a bra, it was to the Bump she confided and knew he heard her heart of hearts.

Little Fay and Hazel, who stepped in and out of each other's ideas as easily as blue jeans, stopped to pay homage to their curious, unknown brother and recognized an arbitrator and a friend.

Fifteen-year-old Gale talked to the Bump much the same as she did to her dad in his less distracted moments. She felt there was an uncritical ear, unreserved loyalty. "What do you think, Bump? Am I good enough for the soccer team?" She expected straight answers from him and got them.

Celia had witnessed her mother's pregnancies three times before, although only with the twins had she been old enough to pay close attention. A few of the girls at school, some younger than herself, had babies of their own. She sometimes felt an overwhelming tenderness toward the Bump, and she knew he was extraordinary somehow. She imagined him merry and rosy with bright curly hair, a laughing kind of baby, with rolls of fat and a little Chiclet for a tooth. Maybe someone from a baby food company would spot him, and he'd be on all of their labels and commercials. He'd be an early talker. One of her friends had a brother named Alfie, who was barely three but spoke like a little old gentleman. He could say the alphabet and recite poems before he was two, and whatever you taught him stayed in his head like a myna bird. "That was a really lovely dinner, Daddy," he'd say, and they'd all crack up. Celia knew the Bump would be exactly like that, and he'd walk before Alfie did, too. He'd be eight months old and lurching around the house wearing tiny high-top runners. She could hardly wait to help buy his clothes. Little shoes were so cute it made her crazy.

"Bathroom is yours, Celia."

She ran past her mother, banged the door shut, then announced through it, "I hate my nose."

"You've got a lovely nose. It's like something you see on old coins."

"It's Dad's nose. I do not want a man's nose. God, old coins? Great. Like Julius Caesar or somebody, big lump on top."

"It's arched, Celia. It's a sign of character."

"I don't want character. I want surgery."

"If you were any more beautiful, you would be dangerous. I don't know how you did it."

Celia crashed out of the bathroom, quickly tying back her hair. "I'm late. Shit. Okay, see you tonight."

There had not been a plan for any of this. Louise, still drowsy from the nap, had the queer sensation of having suddenly arrived in this place, heavily pregnant, landing there to sort through someone's messy kitchen and an evening meal for seven.

Twenty years had somehow dissolved since she'd first met Gavin. Louise would catch a glimpse of herself in the old cheval mirror upstairs—the glass scratched and moody—surprised by the image there, her plump whiteness, stretched and scarred, the skin under her breasts like fine crepe. A body used. Gavin. Five infants. *One day,* she thought, *I had these twenty years in front of me. Nothing had been written. Anything could have happened.* But what *had* happened still left her puzzled. She didn't believe she was stupid or lacked the imagination needed to have made more impressive choices, to have directed differently the events that shaped her life or defined her—whatever that meant. It had just all happened, rolled along while she was too busy to notice.

She turned off the radio and their old house was quiet, a rare thing, so Louise leaned against the counter and shut her eyes to the clutter. But the pup in his pen outside began yipping frantically. Louise smiled at her frustrated hope of reprieve and waited for the slam of the back door and the commotion of twins and dog, whom they would certainly rescue from the lonely yard.

It's fine, she thought as she heard them, and braced herself as they burst in.

Fay's braids had fallen out, leaving one elastic hanging precariously from a little tangle. Ketchup stained the front of her shirt, where she'd wiped her mouth, and her legs had several bruises. Witch Hazel and Fey-Fay. They were identical twins, but in some matters, they must have decided on opposite tacks as if to maintain a certain balance. They were fine-boned, with eyes flecked as agates. The two of them sat on the floor and pulled off their shoes as Louise started dinner.

"We were playing with the Next Doors, and they got a new bike, but Hazel took the water bottle frame off it, and Mrs. Weir got mad at her, right, Hazel? And I said it wasn't her fault she didn't do it on purpose, and she said go home right now, so we did. What's for dinner, we're hungry, right, Hazel?"

"Yup." Hazel's dark hair was still done up in neat French braids. They both wore shorts and t-shirts, but somehow Hazel's looked fresh and ironed, as she herself did.

"Bloody Mrs. Weir," said Fay.

Louise turned from the stove and frowned. "Miss Fay Protheroe, don't let me catch you talking like that again. If Margo Weir wants you out, then you come straight home and don't worry about it." But she thought, *That loudmouth woman is always right, and her goddamned sons can do no wrong.* "And furthermore, where is your book bag?"

"We forgot to hug the Bump."

"Never mind me, I don't need one."

"Hug the mom. Hug the mom." Four skinny arms, four sharp elbows, two pointed chins, two shrieking girls, and a plump woman wearing a lilac tent danced to the music of simmering meatballs.

The Kraken stirs. Innocent, primitive eyes gaze upon unsettling things in its watery cave. Distant currents tug; soft lights flow like oil through the water. It stretches out tentacle arms, questing. The currents pull harder; the Kraken breaks free of its mooring and begins to float. Up and up. All around, tiny fish lights blink on and off, finally disappearing in the cold depths below. The ocean surge carries the massive Kraken without effort. Louise screams. No sound comes.

She woke at four-thirty in the morning with sweat pooled, trickling down her ribs. Her uterus was contracted, not painfully, but enough to take her breath away. Backache. She would wait a while; this had happened many times in her other pregnancies. Labour was real labour with her—there was no mistaking it—something like being simultaneously run over by a truck and kicked in the tailbone by a donkey.

Almost two hours before true morning, a thousand rowdy sparrows visited in the trees outside the window. She got up and went to the bathroom.

Down the hall from Louise and Gavin's room, little Hazel is driving a 1962 Lincoln Continental. Hazel doesn't know that's what it is, only that it is huge and black and has suicide doors. Something is wrong. Snow covers the streets, and there are too many controls on the dash and she can't see out the windshield. The wipers start up. She drives and drives through the streets, silent snow floating down like cotton balls. She pulls over and stops. Why did she stop? She didn't want to.

Someone is behind her now, driving slowly, looking for her. Hide quick. *How do you start a car?* Then the motor is running. *How do you make it go?* Put your foot down. Harder. Put both feet down.

She wants to cry. It creeps along, it is too big, it is sliding around. *Put your feet down hard. Someone is coming, he'll see you. Hurry.* The Lincoln picks up speed, races out of the town and down a road, fast, up and down hills. Faster. She tries to call out, but her voice doesn't work.

In the bed across the room, under a matching Dutch-girl quilt made by their grandmother, Fay scowls furiously in her sleep. She mumbles, "Leave me alone, quit following me, go away. I can't drive, I'm eight years old. Stop the car."

Celia sleeps down the hall from them on a waterbed, the sheets and comforter printed with tiny flowers on deep plum. She'd lain on her back with arms folded across her chest, dark hair spread on the pillow—a lovely corpse laid out for the wake.

She steps from the limousine, linking arms with a handsome young actor. Celia Protheroe, nominated once again for Best Actress, stunning in her simple black gown. Win or lose this Oscar, her photograph will be everywhere. She already has her own line of cosmetics.

NEXT MORNING, Fay brought the newspaper into the dining room. "Hey, where's Mother Louise? Hey, Mom, can we have a spider?"

"You don't have spiders; you step on them or put them outside, depending on how Buddhist you feel. And don't talk about it at the breakfast table. I feel a bit sick."

"Can we keep one, I mean, like a pet? There's lots of kinds for pets, right Gale? They live in aquariums and don't make a mess. I found a kind that eats rats, and rats are no good, they get rabies and stuff, right Gale?" One of her braids, which Louise did for the twins that morning—tartan ribbon included—was already unravelling.

"Only sometimes," said Gale. "Anyhow, that is disgusting. And anything that ate rats would eat you, too, I bet. It would creep out of its cage and suck our blood at night and then procreate all over the place. It isn't a suitable pet for an eight-year-old. Ask for a hamster, Fey-Fay. And fix your hair. If you'd get it cut short as mine, you wouldn't have to worry about all those dopey braids and tangles."

Gavin munched on a bowl of cooked five-grain cereal and requested the classifieds. Gale grabbed the rest of the paper from Fay and read out loud. "Archnophobes need not apply! There is a craze for spiders hitting exotic pet enthusiasts across the country. Distributors say they can't keep up with the demand for one in particular, the giant Goliath. This poisonous pet is thirty centimetres in diameter and has fangs almost two centimetres long. Goliath, also known as *Theraphosa Leblondii*, requires two rats a week and is considered to be a very aggressive specimen. One per cage is the limit for these venomous favourites, who will attack and eat their own kind. Owners can expect the pleasure of Goliath's company for up to twenty years. How do you handle them? Very carefully."

"So, what do you think, Gale?" Should we get one?"

Gale stared back at Fay and said, "You need professional help. But don't worry, Mom and I will sell our bodies to help pay for counselling."

Louise said, "Speak for your own body. Nobody would want mine."

"'Forty-eight-inch above-ground pool, sixteen-foot diameter, liner and pump.'"

"Dad, we're eating, please."

"'Eight hundred dollars o.b.o.' Oh bee oh! It's so stupid. I hate it when they say that."

"We know, Dad, shut up, okay?"

"Paving blocks. Weren't the Weirs looking for some to put behind their garage?"

"Who cares?"

"Here's something for Celia if she ever gets out of bed. 'Wedding dress, train and veil, size six, never worn.' Doesn't that tell you a classic story?"

"Heartbreaking. The bride gained weight."

"Your dad is worried that some poor girl was left sobbing at an altar."

"Look for the ad in a few weeks, 'Wedding dress, never worn, size eighteen.'"

"'Wedding dress, maternity, size twenty, worn once.'"

"Cruel women, how can you laugh at the misfortunes of others?"

"How can you read that crap?"

. . .

"Whose wedding?" asked Hazel. She had not been able to eat a bite since Gale said she would be selling her body.

She got no reply. She turned hopefully to Fay, who could usually explain things on their behalf really well, but she was poring over the Goliath article, sounding out some words. Gavin was deep in the classifieds, and Morgan had just come downstairs, so she was no use.

She turned to her mother but could only see Louise's paleness, the shadow on her face and the deep lines under her eyes. *Something is wrong with everything,* thought Hazel. *Something isn't sitting right.* Hazel was scared to look at Gale, in case her body had changed somehow, so she stared down at the table and said, "I don't get it. If Gale sells her body, then who takes it, and what will we do?"

Everyone looked at her in surprise. There she sat, cold porridge in front of her, back straight as a dancer's, ankles crossed beneath her chair.

"I meant I'd be a prostitute. I was only kidding."

"I think I know what a prostitute is. That's gross."

"It was a joke. And what do you mean, what will we do?"

"Without you. What will we do if you aren't here?" Hazel's eyes filled and spilled over. Tears dripped on the pockets of her white blouse. A drop hung from her nose.

"My God, Hazel, I'm not going anywhere, and nothing is going to happen to me or my body, and if someone tried to make me a prostitute, I'd castrate him on the spot and feed his nuts to Tangent."

Tangent was the pup, a five-month-old Shetland sheepdog. He was especially fierce with brooms and was still not quite house-trained.

Celia had thought of his name, which her family agreed

was inspired, although her grandparents and neighbours could never seem to remember it. Tangent could not sustain a straight line. The girls would kneel down and call him, and he'd hurtle toward their outstretched arms, then abruptly take a sharp right. But at that moment, he was shut in the back porch under house arrest, having made a deposit in the living room before breakfast.

Gavin said, "I'm sure he'd enjoy a chew on someone's testicles while he's out there feeling sorry for himself."

"Really," said Louise.

"Hey, Morgan, you can't sit there, that's Celia's chair."

"Shut up. So where's my place, Fay? You guys are eight years old. You should be able to count by now."

"The laundry's on your chair."

"So where's my glass and everything? Everybody always forgets me. I don't care. I'm sitting in Celia's place. She never gets up on Saturday." Louise set a bowl of hot oatmeal in front of Morgan, who scowled at it and chewed on her lip.

"The reason you're forgotten is that twelve is one of those invisible ages—you should learn to take advantage of it," advised Gavin.

Morgan ignored her dad, made melty brown mountains of sugar in the porridge, and skimmed over its topography in her twin-engine Otter, dipping past canopied rainforest toward hidden valleys.

He continued. "When you're invisible, you can get through life unscathed. As in, 'Morgan could live through this breakfast unscathed.'"

"You need to get taller or louder or something," Gale said to her.

"You'll notice me when I've got my pilot's licence, and everyone wants a ride someplace."

"When we want a ride, Morgan? What, you're going to fly us downtown?"

"No. Like the Amazon or New Guinea—some place with animals that haven't been discovered yet."

"If they aren't discovered, how do you know they're there?"

"Because I'm good in science, that's how."

"Hey, Morgan, you could use your ears to fly, like Dumbo. They're big enough."

"I hate you, Gale. You're such a prick."

"Morgan."

"Sorry, Dad."

"Also, I don't think girls can be pricks."

"Gale can," she muttered. Morgan untucked her short hair to cover the offending ears, but it didn't quite work.

Louise said, "Leave her alone, Gale, she's got sweet ears, she has elf ears, it means she's going to be very special when she grows up."

"I do not have elf ears."

"Don't cry about it, we're bugging you."

Morgan didn't care. She was going to fly one day; she knew it. She already flew at night, arms outstretched and the hem of her dress caught by a thousand birds. Even when she was a very little girl she would dogpaddle through the air, over telephone wires, over the roofs of her neighbours' houses. *I told you I could fly,* she would shout. *I used to think it was a dream, but it wasn't and look at me.*

Louise piled sticky bowls in the crook of her arm, quick as a waiter, carrying enormous loads back and forth, but it felt like this baby was going to drop any minute. She carried him low, and now it sometimes hurt just to sit much less walk. "Did I tell you Myrtle Murray wants to give me a baby shower? Says I deserve one after this bunch, especially since the Bump is a boy. She told me she had a dream about him. I was afraid to ask. But she said he is a true Celt; she saw his second toes, and they were long, and that his face was like those medieval pictures of the sun, bright and surrounded by curls. I said, 'And what kind of dream is that to have about a little baby—couldn't you have dreamt that he'd grow up to be an orthodontist or a gynecologist so he could support his aging parents?'"

Louise stopped and raised her chin, blinked hard several limes, and looked down at her family in perfect imitation of Myrtle. "'Now. this is a boy who is going to like lots of colours, and the shower is on Friday, so come and don't be ungracious!' I wish sometimes she'd keep her dreams to herself." She picked up Gavin's coffee mug and headed for the kitchen.

Fay's elbows had the spider section of the newspaper pinned to the table for safekeeping, and she leaned her chin into her palms. "How does she know he'll like lots of colours?"

"Big deal, all babies like colours. She's trying to be spooky and psychic. And all babies have round faces. I don't think that was such a great dream," said Gale. "I liked the one Mom told us about her husband dying better."

That was last fall. Myrtle Murray had said, "I had the most wonderful dream, Louise. I was in the cutting garden out back, and the day was crystalline. I knew I was in a dream from that, when real becomes so real and perfect, the air so clear that every colour seems true, and I could smell sweet rose, but there was no rose there, just my usual cutting flowers, with evening stock and freesia for scent. Well, I never did have much luck with roses, but nevertheless there was a strong air of rose. And I said to myself, *Someone will die. Someone I love very much.*

"And two nights later, well, early in the morning, really— that's when I do my dreaming—I was walking up many stairs in a strange house. It was very dark, but I wasn't in the least bit nervous, and the stairs seemed to climb and climb, and then I was in a little bedroom. The roof was dormered, and the windows were not glazed but opened right into the night sky, and the stars were huge. Too huge. There was the sound of quiet breathing, a sleeping person. I crept over to the bed, and there lay Edmund. I said, 'Edmund, are you sleeping?' I spoke quietly so I wouldn't startle him, you know, and he opened his eyes and looked so sweetly at me and said, 'No, dear, I've died.' It was so natural, Louise, I knew it was true. And you and I both know how I've been so worried about his heart all these years."

Three days afterward, eleven in the evening, a knock had come to the Murrays' door. Two tall policemen stood there, asked if she was Mrs. Myrtle Murray, removed their caps, came inside, and informed her there had been an accident.

"My Edmund is gone," she'd said to them. "I knew it was coming, but I always thought it would be his heart." And she'd phoned the Protheroes, told them calmly what had happened, and asked them to come with her to identify his body. Gavin waited outside. Midnight at the morgue.

Myrtle had come out, glassy-eyed and smiling faintly, Louise holding her arm. "You know, Gavin, I had half a mind to scold that man for trying to pull one on me. There he lay with his feet bare, his legs all awkward, and his hair a bit of a mess. Why, I've seen him look much worse and drunk as a skunk after a night at the Legion. Poor Edmund, he looked surprised. But can't you see the old fool giggling at the bunch of us crying and carrying on? He'd want to sit up and have a good laugh."

That's true love, Louise had thought, doubting her own parents would launch one another with such humour into ever-lasting life and imagining the hymns her mother would want. "Rock of Ages." "Nearer My God to Thee."

"How come we aren't invited to the shower?" asked Morgan.

"You'd be bored silly, and anyway, you've got school."

Louise thought of her mother again that day as she got out the wash pail. Even now, Rachael never seemed at peace. She had worked as hard for her one child as Louise did for the five girls; maybe that was why she seemed so intent on the prospect of a better life after this—her rest with God, Whom she'd made sure Louise was well aware of. Louise used to love Sunday School, drawing *Daniel in the Lions' Den*, *Joseph's Coat of Many Colours*, singing "God sees the li-tul spa-ro-oh fall." Was it cruel to make children believe "if God so loves the li-i-tul birds, I know He loves me too"? She wasn't convinced the world was really any worse than it ever was; in fact, some things were a whole lot better. She remembered researching an essay for high school and how she'd cried as she read her mother an article about a thirteen-year-old boy hanged in New York City for stealing from a fruit stand. The lad cried piteously as he was led to the gallows, went the account, and Louise had been outraged.

Rachael had put down her mending and said, "Heaven's sake, Louise, it happened a long time ago. No point being upset now." But Louise had known it was good men who'd arrested that boy and good men who'd put him to death.

Gavin would never have told her not to grieve. He would have understood that he might have been that boy himself if he'd been unlucky enough to have been born then. Gavin had a rare tenderness to him, a natural sympathy. Louise used to be a bit embarrassed by the people who approached him sometimes, complete strangers, the sort who seemed out of focus, hanging on the edges. They would start talking to him right out of the blue, in lineups to movies or in stores, tell him about their allergies or the cab ride they just had—odd things.

But she was used to it now. Gavin had once worked in a broom factory, a long time ago when he still thought of saving money for an education. There had been a guy named Andrew, a hard worker, broad-faced, weak blue eyes. He was slow in the head. Every day, he would wink at Gavin, set down the curling broom he was tying, and tell him about his girlfriend. "I'm going to see Theresa on this Friday night," he'd say. "I think I'm gonna get 'That Feeling in the Moonlight.'"

Louise was getting that feeling in the moonlight as she washed the sticky floor, then wondered about a polygamous family she'd seen interviewed on television, how one of the wives of this wholesome-looking man said, "It is a fair arrangement, he never bothers us when we are in the monthly time or pregnant."

Louise brushed off the webs spun by God-fearing people, put on a Stevie Ray Vaughan tape, and planned to make heavily pregnant love to Gavin.

THEY WERE GOING to the farm, all but Celia and Gale, whose homework excused them this time from the ordeal of Sunday supper with their grandparents. Louise stared out the window, Gavin drove, Hazel and Fay—side by side in overalls and plaid shirts—did a dinosaur puzzle, and Morgan read an ultralight aircraft magazine with Tangent curled on her lap, sleeping.

Louise's father, Harold Timmons, was the third generation to work that land but was forced to quit farming a few years after his daughter married. He was then in his early sixties, but already dementia had begun to take him over, and his affliction, as Rachael called it, was becoming not only a hazard but expensive. To his shame, he could no longer estimate the length of a harrow or drill, caught the ends of implements on trees, forgot to bring around the spout of the combine, and spilled grain in the harvest field. So, the land was rented out, and they lived off a share of the crop and their small pensions. Rachael's endless cycle of work had changed little over the years. She still kept an enormous garden, a few chickens, and a small orchard, and put up quantities of preserves.

They drove into the yard and waved to Rachael where she knelt in the narrow flower bed by the house, shaded in her huge straw hat. Gavin pulled in beside Harold, who stood with his back to them, stooped and barefoot, immersed in one of the last warm days of the season.

Rachael came over and gave her daughter a peck on the cheek. "Haven't had that baby yet, I see," she said sternly as if Louise were late returning a library book.

Harold wagged a finger. "Better make this one a boy. Gavin's got too many goddamned women in that house."

Louise wondered how she had ever learned any parenting skills at all.

The twins vanished, already halfway to the garden for

wheelbarrow rides, but Rachael didn't let Morgan get away so easily.

"Hop down to the cellar for me, would you, dear, and bring up a pail of potatoes."

"Do I have to, Gramma? I hate it down there."

"Now, don't make faces, Morgan; your legs are younger than mine."

Morgan grabbed Gavin's arm, tugged him away from her grandfather, and whispered, "You come with me. I can't go by myself; it's haunted."

"You bet it is," Gavin said. "Come, and I'll show you."

Down the springy backless stairs, across ancient linoleum crumbling to dust under their feet, past the wringer washer, laundry tub, and shower stall, which was put in to wash the dirt of the field from Harold Timmons just in time for his retirement. There were three wide doors of tongue-in-groove board, splintered with age, that closed with latches. Gavin opened one of these, and they were in the cold room. They stood a moment listening to someone's footsteps upstairs, *reeka reek* overhead. Morgan looked at the trap door where the potatoes were kept and said, "I'm not going down there."

"Nope, this way." Past dusty shelves of beets, candied crab apples, and spiced beans to the back of the room.

Dr. Frankenstein's laboratory. Instead of brains in formaldehyde, the mason jars were packed tight with waxen-fleshed chickens. Canned hens. Pallid little corpses. "Here's your ghosts," he said. Floating in obscurity since Louise's mother did them up for the last time fifteen years ago. Louise had refused to eat these even as a child.

"Eww, Dad, you are so stupid. I thought it was going to be something really good. This is pathetic."

Gavin got the potatoes.

"How's that bike of yours, boy?" asked Harold when they were safely back outside.

"Haven't had it for a while," said Gavin. He'd sold it for rent money seventeen years ago when Celia was an infant.

"They're good on gas, them things."

"You bet," said Gavin.

Harold turned and walked toward the shop. He held his arms straight out to the side for balance and put one foot deliberately in front of the other. A sock hung from each back pocket. Rachael stomped off after him. "Heaven's sake, Harold Timmons, where do you think you're off to now without your shoes? There's nothing for you to do out there, and Louise and Gavin and the girls are here to see us. Now get back and have your supper. Louise, go get him. He won't listen to me once he's made up his mind." In fact, he rarely listened to his wife. He'd never made a habit of it before and couldn't see a point to it now.

Louise took her dad gently by the arm and steered him back toward the house, talking the whole time. Harold beamed at her, his eyes pale and bright with age. He thought she was wonderful. He deeply respected her but forgot why.

He was looking into eyes and a face very much like that of his mother, who fled prairie farm life back to Ireland when Harold was four years old, leaving him to be raised by his father and grandparents. His father had been a stern man who demanded the respect of hired help and kept the farm going through hard times. But he was not able to keep his young bride and gave what love he had left to his son.

A letter had come for his father from Harold's aunts in the old country. A copper-coloured pony had appeared before his mother, they claimed, and she'd run home white as a ghost, saying it was a punishment for leaving the little one on the godforsaken prairie. Sure enough, she drowned not a week later. Sad for a boy to grow up believing his mother hadn't wanted him, though Rachael said she knew it to be otherwise.

Eighty years ago. Louise sometimes wondered if the kelpies and their kind were there, still, or had they been snuffed out by microwaves and acid rain.

Harold had been well into his forties when he and Rachael married, and Louise was their only child. His own mother had died from a punishment, and Louise was born in punishment, Rachael paying for her own sins as well as Eve's, judging by the difficulty of the birth. Rachael was advised by the doctor to bear no more children, and neither partner needed much incentive to forego their conjugal duties, which Harold was unenthusiastic about due to his age and bachelor habits and she from natural distaste.

Rachael called everyone into the house and got them settled properly. "Would you like to ask grace tonight, Gavin?"

"I asked her already, but she wasn't willin'," said Harold. He stared proudly around the table, mouth open and grinning. They all ignored him; he'd used the same joke every Sunday supper in memory.

"Bless this house bless this meat bless me let's eat," said Gavin. His mother-in-law sighed and passed him the mashed potatoes. It wasn't blasphemy in the strictest sense and tamer than some of his graces, but she was compelled to keep her lips pressed together and stare down snickers from Hazel and Fay.

"Bless me," giggled Fay. Hazel snorted into her napkin, shoulders shaking.

Their grandfather turned to the little twins and said, "I saw that one from town. I saw that girl married that fella." He chewed slowly, carefully. They watched his fork head back to the plate, so slow, and circle like a hawk up against a strong wind over turnip and jellied salad. The suspense was deadly. The fork stopped, hovering an inch above the roast.

Rachael stood up to reach the gravy bowl and winced as she bumped her leg against the chair. "For heaven's sake, Harold, what girl are you talking about? There's lots of girls married some fella."

Harold kept chewing; cleared his throat. The fork speared a bit of meat.

Just don't let Gramma talk about her rotting legs, Morgan thought, *and I will live unscathed through this meal.*

Rachael turned away in annoyance. "Tell me about that math test, girls. Was it as bad as you thought it would be?"

Fay and Hazel complained about it for a few minutes, then Fay transferred her milk moustache to a sleeve and fished around the floor for her napkin. Morgan kicked it out of reach, then kicked Fay under the table. Morgan wished she had a normal family; she couldn't wait for the Bump to get born.

"How're your legs today, Mother?" asked Louise.

"That other vein's been acting up now, the one that burst, you know, and it's got a sore too, all right, but I've been changing the dressing every day. Had the public health nurse come by, and she said now you best watch that in case there's anything unusual, like if the pus doesn't look right, she means, or if there's streaks around the ulcers."

Morgan clutched her fork tight so it couldn't be thrown anywhere like it wanted. She put on what she hoped was a beseeching look and tried to catch someone's attention, but Louise couldn't see her, and Rachael wouldn't quit.

"Well, I've got to watch for blood poisoning, I guess. Remember how Rose's leg got so bad from infection? Of course, she had the diabetes, but it was a real mess. Smelled too."

"May I be excused?" said Morgan.

"Morgan, help clear the dishes. I'll bring in the pie now, Mother."

"The fella with the bees," said Harold Timmons.

"You mean the Stevenson boy. The one who married Rose's girl Edna."

"That's the one."

"Well, what about it?"

"Pass the cream there, Gale."

"I'm Morgan, Grampa."

"Morgan, then."

Rachael thrust back her chair. "Gavin looks like he wants more coffee."

"You bet," said Gavin.

Rachael limped into the kitchen, sighing. *Dear Jesus, give me strength and the patience of your heavenly angels, and if you take me tonight, it won't be too soon for me, amen.*

When Rachael Timmons, nee McTavish, goes to heaven, she will be a little girl forever. She will wear black patent-leather shoes with gilt bows on them, tiny cotton-lace ankle socks, a huge crinoline under the snowiest white square-dance dress you ever saw. There is a rope swing in heaven, and no end to how high you can get on it, and it's no matter if you jump off when the swing is at its highest because you'll land in white sand, soft as marshmallow, and won't get dirty. There is a Ferris wheel, cotton candy, toys and more toys. When you look to the horizon, you will see some gritty smoke. That is Hell. If you walk that way, you will find the Pits, black and oily, and little Rachael's parents sitting there miserably.

LOUISE FILLED the old porcelain sink and put cutlery in to soak. This kitchen was a study in inefficient work space, and though she grew up there, Louise still did not know how her mother prepared these big meals, baked, and put up jars of preserves. There was the little wooden table and the Knechtel Kitchen Kabinet, which Rachael brought with her from her own mother's house. It contained a flour bin, cutting board, bread cabinet, drawers, and shelves. A piece of heavy printed paper was nailed to the inside door. It came with the cabinet when it was new and was now brittle and brown; grease stains obscured some of the print. Louise frequently studied its counsel. Like a knowledgeable aunt, it had lots to say to a younger housewife. "Check your Grocery Needs against this list." She was pleased that a list three generations ago included birdseed, cream cheese, olives, five fruits, and three kinds of sugar. She understood Coal Oil, Stock Food, Mucilage and Crocks, but was confounded by Bath Brick, Oyster Shells, Sulphur, and Sweet Oil.

"Things Worth Knowing and Remembering." How to prevent hairs from coming out of a toothbrush; how to clean ink from linen using lemon juice, yellow soap, and pure melted tallow; how to cut fresh bread, clean chair covers by rubbing with hot bran, cement a loosened knife handle using resin, plaster of Paris, and beeswax; when to bake with sour milk. It made Louise tired to think of it.

Part of the paper was torn away, leaving disappointing omissions in the advice. Like her dad's mind, it was filled with blocks of irrelevant information, fragments of sentences, good ideas half-finished. Louise felt she would suffocate.

"Want to walk a bit, Mother?"

"You go ahead, dear. I'll finish these up."

Louise didn't bother asking anybody else—she could see they were glued to the television. The pup barked in circles around her, some genetic memory compelling him to herd this person. She went past the row of old granaries to the willows that bordered the yard and stared into the setting sky. The westering sun, its light growing long as the days grew short, cast bronze across the prairie and died its nightly dramatic death. She knew why her parents would never move from here.

It hurt to walk. The Bump was so big now that his little kicks and punches rolled into her, took her breath away. She headed out the west gate and leaned against a fence post to gaze across the renter's field of lentils to the distant bluff. The trees changed from green to black as she stood. She turned back to the house, the air a grainy haze, the growing dark like a wrap, pleasant, enfolding.

She came in, turning on lights as she went, although she knew her mother would only turn them off again when they left. Years ago, Gavin had wired in an outside light, which her parents usually forgot about. Often, they'd arrived at the farm thinking nobody was home, and Louise would warn her parents that one of these days, somebody was going to waltz right in, thinking they were robbing an empty house.

Gavin and the three girls were in the living room, tired and irritable. Harold Timmons, fast asleep and upright in the big chair, had a friendly little smile on his face.

On the way home, trying to count telephone poles against the blue-black sky, Morgan realized they never did find out where her grandfather saw the girl who married the Stevenson boy who had the bees.

HAZEL RECLINED ON THE SOFA, eyelids fluttering, kerchief on her head. She raised an arm feebly, rested the back of her other hand against a fevered brow, and said, "Oh, Fair Vasilisa, I am ill and need somethingorother from the forest. Please fetch it for me, and try not to get eaten up by Baba Yaga."

Then she jumped from the sofa, put on a red apron, and skipped around the rug.

Fay was standing in a laundry basket on a chair. "Watch it, here I am zooming around in my mortal and pestle, looking down on my chicken-leg house, and there's my fence made of men's bones. And what else do I see? It's Fair Vasilisa, to grind up for lunch."

"Oh, you ugly old woman, get the hell away from me and don't grind me up. I have to find somethingorother for my mother, who is sick."

"I'm telling Mom you said a swear."

"What do you care? You're supposed to be a witch."

"Play right or don't play. I hate it when you do that."

"Then let me be Baba Yaga."

"You're already a Witch Hazel."

Hazel shrieked and lunged at Fay, caught her by the pigtail, and wrapped it around a fist until her face twisted in pain. "Say 'uncle,' and fast."

"Uncle and fast." Hazel relaxed her grip, and Fay's arms became skinny little pistons, pounding into her sister. The shrieks were deafening.

Gavin stepped around them. "Love and hate, shaping the human condition. And I don't want to know about it, I don't care, so save your breath." They got up in tears, panting and yelling for him to listen, hanging from his arms and legs to anchor him. "Go see how the Bump is doing, but be very quiet and don't let him know you were fighting, or he won't want to be born."

The girls went off to find their mother. *The Bump*, Gavin thought. *That kid has heard more in utero than most kids hear in half a lifetime. What will the girls do when he's born? It's going to be hard to consult a howling nuisance in dirty diapers.*

Gale yelled from down the hall. "Why do you let them act like that? You spoil them rotten! My friends' little brothers don't even get away with that."

A WHILE LATER, Gavin was in the basement creating noises, hollow metallic echoing thumps. *Whumpa whumpa.* Hazel was with him, being the tool holder, and Fay was the gopher. They had thought their dad was going to do something really interesting with ducks, and promised to help him, but were heartbroken to see the ducks were just furnace things. At least they got to see the crawl space under the house. They also got to see Gavin smoke a cigarillo. It made him look so weird, perched on his ladder, the large man with the little cigar clenched between his teeth, his eyes squinting like a pirate's and his words coming out of the corner of his mouth. The basement light was dim, and fragrant smoke curled above their heads, enhancing the girls' sense of mystery.

"I'll tell you a story," he said. "Gopher, first grab the roll of wire on the bench. Tool person, give me the tin snips."

They hurried.

"It happened to my dear brother, Henery."

"You don't have a brother. You don't have a mother or dad or anyone, right, Hazel?"

"Maybe it was my other brother, Geronimo."

"Dad, quit it. Tell a real story."

"This is real. It's my story, so if you want to hear it, shut up and listen. My other brother, Fred, I think he was, yes, it was definitely Fred, was visiting the rugged coast of Wales a few years back. There's hills there by the sea, rich and green in parts and more like mountains in parts, and circus ponies running around in herds. They have cattle as big as prehistoric oxen, with great curved horns and heads like wheelbarrows. Don't make faces, Fay, this is as true as my life, I swear it. Your mother is lovely, but she has prejudiced you. She thinks she is Irish and that the Irish have the market cornered on druids and little people and all that nonsense. Saint Patrick was a Welshman, and they'd as soon forget that or lie about it, and Merlin was the greatest Druid and Welsher than me. There's barely an Irishman who can speak an old language, like good Welshmen do. Anyhow, my brother, what was his name again?"

"Fred!"

"That brother. He was visiting the Welsh coast one autumn. It was bitterly cold. The sea came into the land all the time and made the days grey and sad, and a thick fog came every night, so he had to open the door of his car to see the edge of the lane. That's what they called the road. He didn't live down a back alley; it was down the lane. He was staying with a little old couple. The woman's name was Gwendolyn, and the man was Bran. They lived in a cottage with a straw roof. And all around that cottage were stone walls—tall walls that came up to the house and short walls all over the hills, some making little squares. Fred figured at first they were pens for animals but decided they were leftovers from buildings that people lived in hundreds or thousands of years before.

"One night, they ran out of shillings for the electric meter, and the lights went out. Gwendolyn said, 'Fred, go out and bring in the laundry for me, there's a good big fellow.' Because Gwendolyn was barely four feet tall herself. Smaller than you two, anyhow. Fred went out through the little tiny kitchen, black as night, out of the little, tiny pantry, and into the back yard. The yard was paved with stone—that's how he knew he was finally outside. There wasn't a whiff of breeze. It was a moonless night and would have been black as the mouth of hell, except the fog had rolled in off the sea, and that fog had a faint, eerie light all its own.

"All Fred had to do was bring in the wash.

"He stood on those old stones, listening to the sound of his own heart, and knew he was not alone out there. There was a multitude. Silent, invisible people, older than Red Indians—crowding him, circling, edging closer and closer. He opened his eyes wide as saucers and strained to see them but couldn't. He squeezed his eyes tight together to make them go away and they wouldn't. They moved in on him. And that's how I lost my brother, Fred."

Gavin stepped from the ladder, threw down the spent cigarillo butt, and spread it around the cement floor with the toe of his boot. Fay and Hazel stared at him.

"Now, Girls, I want all of you to pay attention because I am going to show you this tray for three minutes only. At the end of that time, I am going to put a cloth over the tray. Twyla will hand out pencils and paper, thank you, dear, and this prize will go to whoever can remember the most items on the tray."

Louise knew she would enjoy this shower more if it weren't for the distracting sensation of her pelvic bones being pried apart from the inside. Besides, lately, she'd been feeling hopelessly stupid. Gavin threatened divorce if she called him by the dog's name one more time. But she'd gone for the third pee since she'd got there—Louise loved that bathroom, scallops and shells and gold and blue, feeling like a mermaid every time she walked through the door—and had run out of excuses to avoid playing. There she was with the "Girls" in Myrtle Murray's very meadowy house. Peony curtains draped the front window, which overlooked her natural lawn, a horticultural extravaganza of cosmos, yarrow, poppies, Queen Anne's lace, bishop's goutweed, and bachelor buttons. Prints of flowers hung against pansied wallpaper. The guests found it difficult to locate a place for their tea plates, the occasional tables were so decorated with Myrtle Murray's own arrangements of dried flowers mixed with native grasses, cattails, and pussy-willows. They drank tea from bone china cups edged in gold and glazed with fat, purplish roses. Favours for her guests were wrapped in unbleached cotton muslin tied with blue-for-a-boy satin ribbon, speared with a tiny spray of baby's breath.

Louise wondered where Myrtle had found room to put her husband, Edmund, before he died. Maybe he had stayed in the basement workshop, coming up for meals and bedtimes. Now, part of him resided in an ornate brass urn on his wife's bedside table, and the rest of him had been taken by a nephew and wife up north to his favourite fishing lake and scattered about. For an unnerving few months, then unknown to their Aunt Myrtle, the nephew and wife had misplaced Uncle Edmund's remains. He had somehow been stuck in a box marked "Misc. Storage" during their last move and was, appropriately and mystically, revealed to them when the nephew was searching for some trout flies.

There was an interesting assortment of Girls. Mrs. Myrtle Murray, aged seventy-two, breezed among her guests in a floor-length African print robe in vivid shades of red, her lovely white hair pulled into a French knot. Louise's mother, seventy-four, perched like a bird in the large wicker chair, demure and polite, occasionally offered comments to the company. "There never was such a thing as a baby shower in my day," or "She looks chick in that colour, doesn't she?"

Gavin had delivered Rachael to the shower. If Rachael had asked her husband, and if Harold had managed to find a set of keys, he would have wobbled out to the garage, painfully opened the door of their old Rambler, started it up, and taken fifteen minutes to back it out of the garage and pull up to the house for his wife to sit in the passenger's side. There might have been a chance of them making it into the city alive. Rachael had never learned to drive a car.

Rachael used to say, "I have to drive with Father in case he falls asleep." Louise finally hid the car keys. They pretended not to notice but phoned a neighbour or Louise when they needed a ride.

Myrtle's next-door neighbour, Twyla Jarosz, assisted at the shower with much energy and more noise than Louise thought was entirely necessary. Only twenty-seven, she was the most grownup of them all. Louise imagined her as a little girl, always having to be the teacher when she played school, wearing her mother's clothes and practising looking severe at an early age. Her pronouncements had always intimidated Louise: "Ethics should be taught at home. The school is no place for morals:

only The Church can teach them." When Twyla was within earshot, Louise became conscious of her own comments about the Deity, or raising children, or how she casually swore in conversation. Twyla served the Lord in such a fevered and superstitious fashion that Louise feared her occultist powers. Twyla spoke often of The Church, meaning her own denomination only and certainly not the Holy Mother Church.

If Twyla were a Catholic, Louise believed she would have become a nun, but a faulty one, since her sure and powerful belief system would have caused her constantly to challenge her superiors. Twyla's eyes had the light that revealed qualities needed in a good saint, and saints were never moderate. She lived in a world of Capital Letters. Good Works. The Word. Training Children. Sacrifice.

Twyla had come by the Protheroe home once. Since Louise had greeted her on the street a few times, Twyla felt called to bring her to a Ladies' Bible Study.

"I knew you loved the Lord by the way you were so warm and friendly, and I had the strongest feeling in my heart that I should extend this invitation to you."

"Well, no, thank you, really, I'm sorry. I mean, it's not my interest, but how nice you thought of me."

Louise had poured them all some coffee while the visit floundered around inane, messy conversation, made worse by Louise's determined cheerfulness and Gavin's silence. Fay bounced in for a snack and banged down the milk carton, leaving splashes on the counter. She grabbed a balled-up grey cloth out of the wash pail and was about to wipe up.

"Don't use that, Fay, it's the floor rag."

"You'd never catch me spending time washing my floors like that," declared Twyla. "I use a mop. There's only one thing in this world I do on my knees."

Gavin said, "Well, now, I expect your husband appreciates

that." She looked at Gavin kind of funny. He said, "You praying so much."

Louise's Next Door, Margo Weir, was at the shower. Margo was mother to the Weird Boys, Curtis and Colin. These two were at that moment seated in the Grade 4 room and the Grade 6 room, Curtis in a blue-striped polo shirt, Colin in beige, both wearing walking shorts and knee-high socks. Their hair had a lefthand part; their glasses had identical frames. They were intelligent, inventive little boys who found ways to blame any villainy on their friends, not wanting to endure their mother's anger more than necessary. Fay and Hazel played surprisingly well with them. Louise thought the bunch of them believed they had met fellow twins.

There were three other guests: Jane and Dorothy, widows of approximately Myrtle Murray's vintage, and a young and quiet Alice-somebody, recently moved to the neighbourhood. Louise had met them all before at the Talks. The Talks were given by Myrtle's guest speakers, followed by discussion and tea, and had featured such luminaries as a woman who wrote a fascinating book on her missionary aunt, a man who was a self-trained counsellor and guided others to their past lives, and a lean and athletically built lesbian poetess whom Edmund Murray once mistook for the young man who'd just fixed their furnace.

Myrtle Murray collected people. If she didn't know a person, she often knew of them or could name one of their relatives.

"Position yourselves for the memory game." She held up the little sandglass egg timer. "Ready, steady, flex your brain pans, and go!"

They crowded around the tray, chattering, identifying things. Rubber band. Hair elastic. Spring. Measuring spoon. Lip balm. Button. Crochet hook. Shoehorn. Clock sprocket.

Twenty-five items. Margo Weir won. Her prize was a jar of chokecherry syrup, labelled "From the Kitchen of Myrtle," to which the Girls made complimentary noises.

Jane and Dorothy disappeared for a minute, then entered the room to cheers and laughter, wearing paper baby bonnets, bibs, and big diapers pinned over their slacks and carrying between them a blue laundry hamper heaped with the shower gifts. What man, Louise wondered, would be caught dead celebrating marriage and childbirth as women do, by playing children's games?

The widowed babies presented the hamper to Louise.

She unwrapped a great-footed baggy sleeper covered in red, blue, and yellow *Tyrannosaurus rexes*. The Girls chorused, "Awww" as if they'd seen a basket full of kittens.

"Well, they never had such a thing in my day," remarked Rachael.

Louise, as a baby, slept in a crib built by her dad, enclosed by wide wooden slats with spaces between them just the right width for her little head to become wedged, which it never did. Rachael lost a few teeth the year Louise was born, as she'd expected. "Another baby, another tooth" was the saying, and she never connected it with the doctor's advice to avoid milk during pregnancy in order to keep her figure trim for her husband and never knew the little Louise creature would rob its mother's bones to get what it needed.

Rachael adored baby Louise. She grew the garden, pruned the crab-apple and plum trees, embroidered the pillowcases, and slit the chickens' throats for love of her. For more than three years, Louise was an infant, and she viewed the world mostly from the bouncing confines of a huge old baby carriage. Louise said she remembered being old enough to run to the carriage by herself and Rachael lifting her in; she remembered bumping her head on the sun hood and calling for her mother and leaning over the edge of it, dropping her stuffed toys into the dirt.

There is a picture, less than four inches in height and width, black and white, slightly askew. In the background is a storey-and-a-half wood frame house fronted by a little porch, its peaked roof supported by two pillars and scruffy hollyhocks balanced against one peeling side. There is a thin woman posed awkwardly, an arm crooked across her midriff, the hand cupped, the other hand resting on the roof of a carriage. In the carriage is a bright face surrounded by a frilled bonnet and eyelet-cotton pillowcase and lace gown and jacket, so small in the photo it could belong to a doll. There they are.

Rachael would stare at the miraculous sleeping Louise. She embellished her baby daughter's little bed with as many beautiful things as imagination and sewing needle would allow, and when Louise, miracle again, produced five baby daughters of her own, Rachael presented each with a newborn's layette of soft cotton nightgowns and bed jackets and flannelette nursing blankets, which she embroidered herself.

There, in Myrtle Murray's living room, Rachel could only think that it was the worst bad luck to shower an infant with gifts before it was born but would never risk Louise's scorn by saying so. Instead, she brought Louise a reading pillow made in the same manner as the ones in her crib, eyelet-trimmed and climbing roses done with silk thread.

"Well, now. My." This was all the response Louise could muster to the rest of the gifts—cowboy bibs, baby jeans, and blue things. She was uncomfortable and felt a little foolish cloistered in the fan-backed wicker chair. "The Seat of Honour," Myrtle Murray had said. *Silly woman.*

The decorative bamboo pressed painfully into her bony back and had snagged the sleeve of her best cardigan. She wanted to go home. She had nothing to say to these women.

THAT AFTERNOON, while her mother was being showered by Myrtle and friends, Morgan headed home after their basketball game at school, stumbling down the sidewalk arm in arm with her friend Jessica. They laughed so hard they collapsed on lawns, wiped drool from their chins, and laughed harder. Once in a while, they would raise their faces and howl at the six o'clock moon. Jessica, already thirteen, towered over the slight Morgan. Her frizzy, waist-length hair seemed to blow around by itself. They reeled along the way good drunks should on a bar hop, singing, "When the moon hits your eye like a biga pizza pie, that's amoray." Morgan was terrified, and it lent new heights to her voice. She had never actually seen a bar, but that's where they were headed to get Jessica some supper money.

Jessica lived several blocks away with her mom, Carolanne, and sometimes one of Carolanne's boyfriends. Carolanne was an intense person with a short attention span for love, and her men never stuck around very long. She worked at a dental office downtown and, it being Friday, headed after work to the neighbourhood bar, the main business of the Barclay Hotel.

They stood outside the door, listening to muffled bass pumping out of the jukebox. Morgan was glad the entrance was on the side street.

"What if we get arrested?"

"Come off it, why would we? I've done this lots, it's no big deal. Don't be such a wimp—we're just gonna see Carolanne a minute."

Morgan tried to visualize Mother Louise in there but couldn't. She imagined it would be reeling and raucous inside, with a big silver ball spinning from the ceiling, pool tables, and lots of smoke. Maybe some fights. "We can't go in there."

"Just knock."

"No, you."

"One, two, three." Two fists thumped hard. Amazingly, the door opened.

A young guy in a cowboy hat peered out at them, bouncing his head unsteadily to jukebox Garth Brooks, and said earnestly, "Oh, sorry, girls, was it locked?"

Morgan made a kind of gagging sound. Jessica rammed her with an elbow and said, "No, we're looking for my mother." They stepped in, and daylight vanished behind them. The guy turned back toward the tables and yelled, "Mo-om!" All the women turned around. Morgan felt her face blaze and looked away.

Hey, it wasn't so bad in there, kind of dim and pretty, the bar like a fairyland, with rows of bottles shooting sparkles, little neon signs in pink and gold. Then the bartender glanced up, and anxiety stabbed Morgan's gut. But he looked away and started to wipe off the counter. It was great, like in the movies, a bartender wearing an apron and wiping the counter.

Carolanne muttered, "Oh, shit, it's the Odd Couple." She stubbed out a smoke, then retied her ponytail before coming over with her purse.

"Ten bucks okay, dear? Has Mommy had that baby yet, Morgan? No? Better scoot now, Jess. Love you." She had a row of gold studs in each earlobe, and her brows were plucked into tiny brown crescents. In the earthy red glow of the bar, she hardly seemed older than Celia.

Morgan was beginning to like it in there. Pretty glasses sitting on little paper coasters, brown and green bottles, tiny napkins, party peanuts in wicker baskets.

"Morgan, what're you doing? Let's go."

"I thought you said it was all right we're here."

"You're so stupid."

"Hey, Carolanne, who's your little friends?" Morgan looked over at a table of men, and the one who'd said that was not exactly what she'd call smiling at them. This was something totally new. She hated it. Now, the bartender was looking at Carolanne like he was about to say something.

Morgan backed up and stepped on Jessica, who pinched her arm and muttered through her teeth, "Let's go. Now."

Carolanne glared at the girls. It was a subdued walk to the Lucky Dollar store.

SOMETIMES, a thing happens to Gavin Protheroe's family where their felty thick layer of attachment will suddenly shred and twist in on itself and, in the flash of a moment, they are reeling. Faces transform, teeth clench, fists tighten, and feelings move at fibre-optic speeds. Things best left unsaid are screamed out.

He never knew what started it. Maybe it was him, maybe Louise, maybe their kids. If a camera was aimed at his house, he feared they would all be seen as insane, the girls would be taken into protective custody because normal children couldn't say those things, and normal women don't insult their men like that, and if he was any sort of regular dad, he'd keep things under control; he wouldn't get treated like that. He could never make things come out right, sounding to himself like an imitation of someone pretending to be a real guy. *Pick that junk up right now, or there's going to be big trouble.*

Gavin found himself stunned and depressed on the periphery of his own life, wondering how he got there again.

Louise could be such a bitch. She knew exactly where to stick her comments to do damage. Gavin was six foot two, still well-built though he'd bulked out quite a bit over the years, but Louise didn't know her own strength. *Like a spider ruling the bloody world,* he thought, surrounded by their girls who rallied to her side, supporting her in everything, even stupid things, like because they knew the roar of stadium noise on television drove Louise nuts, one of them would inevitably march in and demand, "Does Mom know you're watching sports?"

Gavin was a natural parent. He approached it in the only way he knew, by not aiming for anything in particular. He fathered by intuition and common sense and was big and comfortable and constant to daughters who grew up jumping all over him like an old couch. There was nobody he cared about in his life to tell him otherwise—to tell him what a father might or might not be.

It was perfectly ordinary to the girls to have no family on their father's side. *He's an orphan*, they'd say. They made so much commotion of their own there never seemed to be a lack of relatives.

He had struggled through school, escaping the notice of most of his teachers, except those who caught him reading books that weren't assigned to the class and were perplexed for a while before forgetting about him. He once had vague plans for going to university but ended up caring for Louise and the babies instead. Sometimes, he felt as if he'd been caught in some great centrifuge and then flung out, separate and spinning.

And would eventually stop in moments of calm. Or perfection, even. Making love to Louise sometimes, telling stories or playing with the girls sometimes, cooking up huge pancakes some Sunday mornings. Then this thing would start up again, and he was never sure where he'd land.

He was nineteen when he'd run into a couple of underage cowboys at the Barclay Hotel. One kid drunkenly tried picking a fight, but the other sized up Gavin and pulled his friend off him.

"No offence taken, man," Gavin had said. The two bought him beer, did great take-offs on Willie Nelson and Waylon Jennings, and, to further impress him, invited him out to a party, one of their open-ended affairs happening most weekends either at the gravel pit or the sand hills fifteen miles east of the city. These boys went to school in a small town nearby where, as it happened, so did Louise Timmons.

Gavin wasn't aiming to get laid; promised himself he wouldn't, though it was hard not to a couple of times. He rode a motorcycle and had that seductive mystique of the slightly older guy around teenage girls, but he was not interested in post-sex entanglements. The girls he went with all wanted love and more love and promises. He never saw the point to any of it until he met Louise.

He had driven out to the hills that weekend, locating the party easily from the noise and the bonfire, and found a scene that was a bit young and frantic for him. He noticed Louise immediately, her unfashionably fair skin almost glowing in the twilight, thick hair tied in a loose braid, and Louise looked back at him with cool green eyes, the same way she watched her friends, removed somehow, not condemning, just not quite with them all. She looked as if she didn't need a thing. It made him pretty hot. He ignored her completely.

He endured several of those parties before he saw her again, but there she was, sitting like royalty on a poplar log, beer bottle in hand, her face fixed on the fire. That time, he didn't play any games; just walked right up and started talking. It was so easy, easier than talking to anyone he'd ever known, and he knew he would die if he lost her.

Less than two years later, they got married. It was the only way he could be sure she'd stay with him.

Now Louise was crying, big wet sobs that made him mad. She deserved to feel bad—her mouth should be a registered weapon. He stomped into their room, where she was curled up on the bed, her nose all red and lips and eyelids puffed out. He'd seen her look better.

He said, "What's your problem?"

"I hate this place, I hate you, and I don't want to live here. If I had anywhere to go, I'd be there."

"I'd be there first."

"Fuck you."

"You speak excellent French. Are you making dinner tonight?"

"Fuck dinner."

"I'll take you out."

"Okay."

Celia knocked at the open door. "Are you guys finished fighting?"

"Are you?"

"I guess. You should never have had us all. It's stupid. I'm not going to have any swarm of kids. Maybe one. And not until I can afford a nanny."

"Your husband might run off with her," said Gavin. He grabbed Louise's wrists quickly.

"A big fat ugly nanny, a grandma, from some Central American oppressed, repressed place that she'll be grateful never to go back to, and she'll adopt me and the baby and teach me Spanish. And who said anything about a husband?" Celia posed herself siren-like against the door.

"Look after dinner tonight, okay?"

"I've got homework."

"Starve, then. I'm taking your mother out."

"I'll make macaroni." She glided down the stairs, pleased with herself.

Hazel and Fay came in the kitchen door, followed by the Weirds.

"Hold it right there. You guys keep it quiet, and whatever you do, steer clear of Louise and Gavin," warned Celia. Little Curtis and Colin took her very seriously, having had lots of practice with evasion tactics in their own house. Their voices dropped, and shoulders hunched a little as they took off their shoes and left them in a precise line by the door. For a moment, Celia considered giving them some dishes to do but thought it would be taking unfair advantage.

"Our mom's having the Bump really soon," confided Hazel, "and Dad says it makes her really bitchy."

"Don't say that word," whispered Curtis.

"Which one?"

"The B one."

"You're such sucks. I bet you guys don't even know how you got born. We know everything. Even periods," said Fay. "Ever wonder why there's no more kids at your house?

Voices dropped to mumbles for a while until Colin shrieked, unable to contain all this explosive information. Celia stormed back into the kitchen. "Out. Outside this second, all of you little morons."

Curtis and Colin were white and shaky as they put on their shoes and glanced fearfully toward the ceiling.

Ten minutes later, as Gavin was helping Louise into the van, Margo Weir opened her front door and stepped over to their driveway.

"Our children have just had a little conversation, I hear," said Margo Weir sweetly. She had on a very lovely smile, the one Gavin called 'I mean no harm, take me to your leader,'

and she crinkled her eyes together just so. "I'm sure you must have heard them in your kitchen, discussing sex and things?" She said it like a question.

"Not at all," said Louise. "But I'm sure it was nothing more than what they learn in health class."

"Oh, I don't know about that." Margo's smile was bigger and stiffer—her eyes were veritable squints. "It sounded a little offbeat to me."

Why did Louise always feel like she was under scrutiny? Was all this guilt normal? Were mothers supposed to report to each other all the time, or did it only happen to her? Thank God it wasn't Twyla Jarosz's kids, not that she'd ever let them visit the Protheroes. But Margo wasn't even religious. What was the problem exactly? She couldn't see it. What in hell was she supposed to say? Had a crime taken place? Was there a proper response?

"Nice talking with you, Margo," said Gavin.

He drove away.

"A bit abrupt, wasn't it? I mean, I'm the one who spends all day long at home; I'm the one who has to face her all the time. Couldn't you have been a little diplomatic? Do I have to be the one every time to deal with all this crap? What did she mean, 'offbeat'? Does she think our little girls are into weird sex? She's such a control freak, I can't stand it."

Gavin's moment of triumph was evaporating.

"Drop it, Louise, it isn't worth it. She's a stupid woman."

"Not really."

He glanced at her. "You're looking a little rough over there, like you've been on a bender."

"No such luck."

"You don't even know what a bender is. You think you're tough, Louise Timmons."

"Not really."

"Did I ever tell you about Roland's grandma's hot feet?"

Silence.

He gave up. The last couple of years, they had discussed sterilization, but it sounded so final and grotesque—vasectomies, tubal ligations. He felt awful thinking it, but he really wished Louise hadn't got pregnant this time. He had reassured her after that night, several times, that she wasn't pregnant, it would be too much of a fluke, don't worry. But she knew. She always knew. Nine years ago, she dreamed about having twins even before her test for Hazel and Fay came back positive, and she was annoyed at Gavin for being surprised. "You know I'm like a damned pinball machine; you should have that figured out by now."

Gavin adored his daughters as babies and adored them more now.

But it was mostly worries, mess, and more worries, and he could hardly find a foothold in his life as it was, and now, just as the little twins were finally growing up, here came one more. And Louise looked like hell.

THAT EVENING, after her fill of rice and black bean sauce was beginning to wear off, Louise announced she was going to the store.

She walked along the quiet street, listening to the soft scuff of her shoes weave into the filtered tune of a child's piano practice. The air was sharp and exhilarating, a mid-September moon was waxing at the half, and Orion's belt glittered bright beyond the street lights. She looked for Cassiopeia, knowing everything was going to be fine; the Bump would join the rest of them like the other babies had, like he'd always been there. It was not a big deal.

Louise fleetingly puzzled over her high spirits, then decided they were produced by following up a big fight with loads of Chinese food and, in anticipation, a Mars bar from the drugstore.

She had gone a few blocks to the east, where the neighbourhood wasn't quite as untroubled, gardens tended to be spare and patchy, the houses older and neglected. Half a block ahead of her, a person came out of his yard and headed toward the main street, as she was. It appeared to be an older man, thin and a little unsteady on his feet, and he seemed to be carrying something. She slowed her pace—although she had no trouble keeping a distance as it was—heeding her mother's warnings to Avoid Drunken Men. It seemed that's what he was, but Louise was comfortable with him meandering ahead in the dark; she could hear him singing quietly as he bent over the thing in his arms. The sound died away as she lagged behind.

She stopped for a moment to look at the house the man had left. A porch light dimly illuminated its veranda windows, entirely covered with what looked like old shower curtains. The front door was almost overgrown with vines, and she smiled at the signs tacked beside it: *no TrespassiNg UndeR no ciRcumsTances* and *Use BacK Door*. He probably lived in a small town once; she imagined him as an old bachelor eating out of tins, with a scruffy piece of furniture that would be parked in the front room to block the door that was never used.

Louise looked up the street to the glow of the big drugstore and saw the man turn toward it. She followed.

She found him there, talking with a young clerk whose badge said *Helen*. It was obvious Helen knew him—got a kick out of him. He seemed to Louise such a gentleman in his tatty old suit jacket, and he spoke in a slow and level drawl.

Helen put the man's mouthwash on the counter and petted the dog he held, a gangly German shepherd-cross puppy, all legs and feet. "So, Wilbur, what's your pup's name?" she asked him.

"He don't have one yet. Anyhow, this here's my seein' eye dog. I need 'im 'cause I'm too pissed to see a thing."

Helen laughed and stroked the pup's ears. It whined and slowly wagged its tail against Wilbur's arm.

As Helen handed Wilbur the mouthwash, he smiled at pretty Louise, who stood plump and hugely pregnant, waiting to pay for a chocolate bar.

Then Wilbur felt one of his dizzy spells coming on. He hoped he could get out of the store before it hit him.

The pup slipped out of his arms, landing on the floor with a grunt, unharmed. Wilbur looked over at the Bump, who gazed right back at him with unborn eyes, sweet as pie and upside down, and Wilbur said, "Well, I'll be damned."

Helen screamed. The pharmacist came running from the back of the store. The two of them bent over the crumpled man, yelled at him, patted his face.

Louise was stunned. She leaned against the counter for a moment, then said, "Phone him an ambulance."

Wilbur Hancock lay on the cold floor, quite dead.

His puppy was sniffing a basket of gumballs.

Louise stood staring, tears running down her face. Her shoes were suddenly wet inside. She said, "Phone another ambulance."

LOUISE CAN HEAR SCREAMING. On and on. Why don't they do something to make it stop?

It is her own scream.

She is floating in a hot night sea, the colour of old red wine, listening to voices, intense nightmare voices that say things in a language she knows but makes no sense. The sea is still.

She lies motionless, eyes wide and staring upward to a circle of brilliance—the sun dogs, burning cool light. Her legs are spread, vulnerable, unchaste; her life is ebbing from the woman's wound, which is truly a wound. In a sea of her own blood she watches now as silent bug people, masked and slip-pered, run around; one is carrying Dion. He is the Blue Baby. He is the Gnome. He is limp and maybe dead. Louise is serene; she might be dead, she doesn't know. A tube is put in Dion's mouth, another is going into his umbilical cord.

She goes past the sun dogs and watches three green people change the bed she lies on. The sheets are red. She follows the bug people around the room, gazes at the blue Dion, his eyes swollen oriental-shut in a face pretty as those of her daughters. She dispassionately searches for life.

A bag of blood hangs from a rack beside the bed; blood flows through a tube piercing the back of her hand.

Louise. Louise.

Shut up, you'll disturb the nanny goat. Look at her, snowy white hair lying in feathers down the knobby back . . . shh . . . watch.

There is a balloon emerging from between the nanny goat's hind legs and she nudges it, a pale silk balloon, bleeding and magic, for inside is a tiny curled-up kid, white as doves. The nanny looks over its shoulder and says in a clear woman's voice, *I love you, Louise.*

Her mother is calling from the house. Louise is sad. She doesn't want to go in yet, doesn't want to miss anything. *I want to watch the kid be born, wait.* The balloon has broken free and falls gently to the weeds. The sac is misty and thick about the tangled limbs of the tiny kid who has turned the tint of morning sky, tinged with blue, and then steadily into the colour of thunderstorms.

The nanny licks away the caul from its head, but when the kid struggles up on wet limbs, Louise sees it has no ears or eyes and its mouth has been sewn shut.

RACHAEL TIMMONS HAD NOT LEFT Louise's side since late the evening before. Maternity wards had changed from the prisons they once were. It used to be that all the babies were stacked onto carts, rows of warm, rounded bundles in white linen. At feeding time, nurses trundled them down the halls to their mothers, and if one or the other wasn't ready, well, they had to tough it out. Nobody but doctors, nurses, husbands, and cleaning ladies ever saw the mother. Rachael had no memory at all of Louise's birth; she was knocked out during the whole affair.

Louise's mother had known at Myrtle Murray's shower that she was witnessing a great wrong, all those foolish women giving presents to a child not yet born. It was one thing to have gifts ready; she certainly made sure each of her new grand-daughters was well provided for, even the twins—God bless them—and good thing Louise had had some warning there would be two, or Rachael would have been short some jackets and things. At the shower, Rachael Timmons could have told those ladies something, though she was somewhat embarrassed all the same for entertaining such superstitions. But she knew that on the one hand, there was God, who cared for your ever-lasting soul, and on the other, there were gods. The gods were the ones who'd make or break you in this world; you never tempted them by showing off your baby, calling attention to it, before it was born alive and whole and breathing. If there was one thing she understood, it was being a mother. Louise alone was hers and was her great contribution, her glory, the vindica-tion of her life. It was so hard not to ever tell her that.

Louise would sometimes say she remembered how, seven-teen years ago, Rachael sat on the edge of the hospital bed and cradled a swaddled, puffy-eyed baby Celia, and she was surprised to see her mother was beautiful. At that moment, with her colourless hair netted in a loose bun and narrow face radiant with affection for her new granddaughter, she had been transformed, exquisite.

Rachael spoke quietly as she brushed her daughter's hair and was careful not to tug. She knew Louise was tiring, so she made a loose braid and helped her lie back against the pillows; for the first time since she was a child, Louise needed her mother. Louise stared at her lap, clutching and unclutching a corner of the blanket; her face seemed muted—the lips drained of colour, eyes drawn tight with pain.

"And now you have your son, you have Dion," said Rachael.

"Dion is a mess."

"He's blessed. They always are; God gives battle to those He loves the most." She tidied things on Louise's bedside tray and thought, *If it was you who'd been taken from me, I would have died.* "There were so many times as you sat in the kitchen with your homework. I worried at you studying so much, but I would never tell you because I knew you were so strong, and you'd mock me for it. You were a funny little thing; it was like you never really needed parents. You could have brought yourself up."

"I don't think you understand what I am saying. My little boy is wrecked. He will never be right."

"I know exactly what you're saying. I would have known by just looking at the little fellow. I'm not you, Louise. I was taught different. It wasn't proper to have too much emotion, not any kind. I remember being at a Valentine's dance with my girlfriend Thelma, and we saw Barry Donnell there with a scorch mark the shape of an iron on the back of his shirt. And of course we knew right away his ma was in her cups again, and so we got the giggles. My mother could shut up just about anybody with a single look, and she did just that for us. I was allowed to laugh, but too much was a sin. Do you know, the only time I ever saw my mother cry was the day she lost the Blue Baby."

"The Blue Baby," said Louise softly.

"Mama delivered it in her own bed, same as she did me, with the help of the midwife, but it was born blue all over. It lived for almost two weeks. I guess nowadays, the doctors could have done heart surgery or something."

Louise could see it: a huge old bedroom with waxed fir floors, the old iron bed with its nubby spread, walls of heavy yellowing paper, a crucifix, and resting under the heavy covers, her young grandmother—jaw set tight and eyes hard as onyx—and nestled beside her, the tiny lavender child, struggling for breath.

"I was sitting under the kitchen table hiding the cat and eating a peanut butter cookie, and you were talking to someone about the Blue Baby, but I thought I'd made it up," said Louise. "For years, I had an image, almost a vision, of a gnome or a fat blue cherub, and it frightened me so much, and here it was really my infant aunt."

"The Priest christened her Veronica."

"Funny, I've seen Veronica growing in Myrtle Murray's rock garden, spiky stuff with blue flowers."

"He named her for Veronica, who wiped the face of Our Lord. He was only a priest, Louise. He was doing a job, and it's hard enough for any man to understand how it is with a mother and her child. Lots of women lost babies in her day. Even in my day."

"Even in my day," Louise echoed bitterly.

"People carry burdens you'd never guess. People have their misfortunes, and some pack them away and never let on anything happened, and others curl up and die from the pain. Or they carry on and try to make the best of life. Take Myrtle Murray."

Louise looked up. "What about her?"

"She had a loss, you know. But it was the kind that everyone hushed up. She had a little one on the wrong side of the blanket. I knew her back then, but we pretend I didn't. She was a nice enough girl, I suppose, but she made a mistake and was sent away to stay with relatives—mind you, no relatives I'd ever heard of. The really sad thing was she never had another when she married Edmund Murray. I don't know if he had a problem or if something happened to her when she had the first. That's her secret and her load to bear. I think about it, though. I try not to, but it can't help but come to mind when I see all these things she grows; it's as if she believes so many thousands of plants might equal one little babe. And I feel for her shame."

Harold Timmons shuffled slowly into the room, trying valiantly to maintain his posture so Rachael wouldn't scold him in public. Gavin held his elbow. "Here's the little guy, Harold, here's Dion. I think he's a real Timmons, don't you?"

Harold peered for a moment into the sleeping face, then shrugged and said gruffly, "Couldn't say. Babies are like pigs and Chinamen. They all look the same to me." The same response he'd given each of his granddaughters.

Louise looked up to see Gavin smiling back at her.

Harold considered Dion once again. "Well, blow me down. He seems like a smart enough little fellow. Are you sure there's nothing can be done for him?"

Louise said gently, "No, Dad, they tried really hard, but there's been some damage."

"Too bad. Damage, eh? Well, now, that brings to mind."

They waited expectantly for a moment, then turned away. Harold was back somewhere in his head, playing hopscotch with memories.

"Doesn't Harold look nice? I cut his hair for him the other

day. He liked that. He just loves to be fussed over," said Rachael.

Gavin said, "I had to stop at the hardware on the way over; needed a washer for the tap, that's why we're so late. I couldn't leave Harold alone in the van; he might find some good-looking girl to run off with, isn't that right, Harold? So he came in with me to have a poke around, maybe find some bargains."

Harold's jaw was in a position usually reserved for sleeping people, relaxed and hanging slightly open. All these nice attentions inspired him to give his daughter a big, slow grin.

Louise leaned rigidly against the pillows and closed her eyes. These conversations had an unwelcome clarity. They intruded like the rubber baseboards and pale uniforms of nurses—details of a world she had resisted but where she was gradually forced to return. There seemed a falseness to the lowered voices and soft steps from the corridor, the buffered thump as Rachael closed the bedside drawer, the sugar-cabbage smell of an approaching food cart.

"Gavin, for God's sake, get them out of here. Now. Take them for coffee, get them out of here. Call the nurse; I want Dion in the nursery. Now. Gavin." Louise shuddered, her breath caught in raging gasps. "I'm going to throw up."

Rachael grabbed the kidney basin and held it for her.

Louise vomited again and again in great harsh convulsions, sobbing while the pain ebbed from her gut, sour and burning, tears splashing down her face.

"Poor little Louise, my baby, don't worry, he's a lovely little one and he'll be fine, shh. My good girl." Rachael stroked her forehead, and when Louise was emptied even of bile, gently washed her eyes and face, and stayed beside her until she was asleep.

TWO

October
———————

> *See see my playmate*
> *Come out and play with me*
> *And bring your dollies three*
> *Climb up my apple tree*
> *Slide down my rainbow*
> *Into a pot of gold*
> *And we'll be jolly friends*
> *For ever more, more*
> *More, more*

Fay and Hazel sat cross-legged on the frosty lawn, facing each other. They chanted loud and fast, complicating the claps and motions, louder and faster, ending in squeals and tangled hands and arms and falling backwards, rolling their eyes in pretend fits.

"What're you guys doing?" asked Colin.

"Did we invite you into our yard? Did you invite the Weirds, Fay?"

"I don't recall inviting you here. I don't like you anymore.

You're sucks." Hazel wanted to add, *and your mother's a bigger one,* but she knew they'd tell Margo Weir what she'd said, and she had ways of making their lives hell without actually doing anything wrong; they could never figure it out.

"What're you playing? Want some?" Curtis pulled red licorice ropes, a bit furred, from a pocket. The girls grabbed one and pulled it in two.

"Insanity," said Hazel. "We're playing schizoid nuts at the funny farm, totally crazed and needing to beat on boys. Want to play?"

"Guess so." The girls looked gleefully at each other and set to. Ten minutes later, they had more respect for the Weirds, who managed to be completely and wonderfully insane without drawing much blood from the girls, and they didn't even cry when Fay and Hazel did their worst.

"Can we see Dion?" panted Colin.

"Hospital."

"Again?"

"Let's play statues."

"Not it."

"Not it."

"Not it."

"It."

Morgan was inside on the phone as usual with Jessica. They were together every possible minute at school, and Morgan tried hard to spend lots of time at Jessica's place, where they were usually alone. It was like playing house. Jessica ate what she wanted when she liked, went where she wanted with whom she liked; she could clean house, write cheques, cook a little.

"No, you've got to come now," Jessica said.

"It's almost six, I can't; we're going to have dinner. Dad's going to be home right away."

"So? Just come, it'll be fun."

"Come on, I can't leave because Carolanne's stupid boyfriend feels like dancing."

"Shit. Don't tell them that. Say I invited you for dinner, and we're going to work on a report or something. Hurry up. I can't dance with him the whole time, and he's bugging me. Just until Carolanne gets back. Please, Morgan. Tell them anything. I'll take you to Dairy Queen after."

Morgan heard the urgency but didn't understand it. She told Celia, who was left in charge for the day, that she'd be eating at Jessica's, and Carolanne was treating them because they had a project to do.

Jessica lived about ten minutes away. Morgan wheeled her bike around back and could hear the stereo through the kitchen window, playing one of those songs everyone's parents seemed to know. Great. She felt really stupid. First of all, she didn't know how to dance, and anyway, how was this going to be fun?

There was no railing on the back steps, no bell at the door, no fence behind the yard. It wasn't much of a yard, either. An old Volkswagen Beetle had been parked there forever in the ratty grass, its windows knocked out and tires flat. Morgan ducked a sagging clothesline to get to the door and knocked a couple of times before Jessica came. Greg was right behind her.

Greg was thirty, lean and stringy and long-muscled like he was used to lots of hard work. She'd met him a couple of times before and thought he was really nice: always talked to them, gave them a bit of money, made a lot of jokes that she laughed at to be polite.

"All right, look who's here! It's little Morgan. C'mon in, little Morgan, let's party." He gave her an exaggerated handshake and spun her around. Morgan smiled up at him as he pranced, and the more embarrassed she got, the harder she smiled. She wanted to laugh at him with Jessica, but Jessica was looking at Morgan like she was angry with her. Then she caught Greg's medicinal breath and saw the empty beer bottles beside the sink. And Greg's eyes glittered, and his lids slouched like a sleepwalker's. He grinned crookedly at Morgan from a face that was not his own.

Now Jessica smiled hugely and yelled, "Let's go, Uncle Greg. To the dance floor." His head swung around, and he followed her into the living room, hands stretched toward the long strands of hair that floated behind her.

"You're a beauty, miss. You're prettier than your mom, and I'm going to dance you to death. And take this little pixie person fairy girl with me." He turned and grabbed Morgan's hand, yanking her along, and already his feet were stamping and hips were swaying. Greg was doing things as he danced that made her think of dogs. She desperately wanted it to be a joke, but it was awful. She danced.

Some of the time, it seemed that Greg was in his own world, rocking alone with jaws clenched and eyes shut; then, possessed by a rowdy inspiration, he'd stomp crazily around the room, trying to connect his moves with the girls'. Morgan danced clumsily, on and on, hopelessly. Jessica moved with a wild energy like she was going to have fun or die in the attempt, and Morgan tried to emulate her, laughing a bit, impossibly trying to talk to Uncle Greg over the music.

And then, the unthinkable happened. The world tipped sideways, her feet were off the ground, and there were arms under her, something her dad used to make happen when she was a little girl, secure and spinning strong, and it would be wonderful. The dancing Greg carried her away from the music and toward the bedroom, and she became disoriented, drifting into that place near the end of the nightmare, waiting for the really bad part to happen so she could wake up. It was crazy. *Stop it. Stop it.*

"Put her down, Greg. I want to dance. Let's go. Come on, Greg, show me that one you did with Carolanne."

Morgan was set down, forgotten for the moment.

"Dance, Morgan, what's the matter with you? Hey, Greg, Morgan's a good dancer, eh? I told you she would be. I bet Carolanne's gonna want some dancing when she gets home."

Morgan felt more trapped by her friend than by this man. She understood now, somehow, and would not leave. Three more times, Greg lifted her into his arms, and Jessica was there talking to him like he was a child and leading him back to dance.

"Hey, Uncle Greg, keep your dancing shoes warm. Carolanne's coming home pretty soon."

"So where *is* the bitch?"

"Let's find you a beer, Greg. Morgan, go find him a beer." Morgan headed for the kitchen. She felt like she was walking in knee-deep water: the aqua walls, the fluorescent kitchen light. She opened the fridge—milk and mustard and hotdogs and margarine and spotted lettuce, and in the door, many brown bottles. Just as she struggled to twist off the cap, Carolanne walked through the back door. She glared at Morgan and said, "That better not be for you."

"Greg."

Carolanne kicked off her shoes and headed into the other room. Morgan followed meekly behind.

"You're fuckin' late enough. Where were you?"

"Nice to see you too, Greg. Jess, get your little friend out of here. I'd like to have some peace in my own house when I come home from work."

Jessica took Morgan to the Dairy Queen; she didn't forget her promise. It was almost eight-thirty. They sat across from each other in a cold booth by the window, watching silent traffic drive through their reflections. There didn't seem to be much to talk about. "I've got to go home. I have stuff to do for Home Ec," Morgan finally said. "You finished your burger?"

"I can't go yet."

"How come? Oh."

"Yeah. Oh."

"I've got to go—they'll call your place for me if I'm late."

"What's stopping you?" Jessica looked at Morgan like she was somebody she'd just met, and then her eyes drifted away, remote.

Morgan wanted to ask. She wanted to ask everything, but Jess would say, "What in hell are you gabbing about Morgan? You're so stupid." She knew that Jess was on the verge of hating her, but if Morgan kept her cool, she might eventually be forgiven.

"Maybe see you tomorrow." Morgan got no reply.

She left by herself, went round the front of the restaurant to grab her bike, parked where she could keep an eye on it. She waved up at the window, but Jessica's head was turned away.

Morgan's face was tight; salt and onion from the meal soured in her gut as she rode off, away from the lights and traffic, into the dark of a residential street. She began to shiver in the autumn evening, so pedalled faster. Her head ached from the cold, from the strangeness. Jess had begged her to come over; how was it possible she'd done something wrong? She thought of the robin she'd found last June dead in the gutter. The memory sickened her.

She'd cradled it in her Cleveland Indians cap all the way to school, so pleased with herself. The classroom was still empty as she had helped herself to a scalpel, microscope, tweezers, jars. She'd positioned the plump bird, planning the first incision, how to carefully peel the skin, keeping the skeleton intact.

Only when the scalpel was in her grip did she truly focus on the robin. Its head hung limply from a broken neck, one eye crushed, the other dull as mud. Seized by fear the bird was alive, she spread its wings and carefully blew on its face to give it one last chance. But instead of a sign from its tiny ribs, there was the flicker of another movement.

She lifted the brim of her favourite cap and stared inside. It was swimming with lice. Vengeance on Morgan the grave robber, caught in the act.

She pushed bird and cap into the garbage and covered everything with bunched-up paper.

All day, she was miserable, and it stained her sleep that night—the horror she had almost committed to one of the creatures who held her aloft in dream flight. Morgan , the despoiler, hoping to wrest secrets from that which should have been left alone.

After that, she had made regular offerings of suet and millet and sunflower seed and kept silhouettes of hawks taped to windows so birds wouldn't crash into the counterfeit sky. *Forgive me, birdlife, for I have sinned, and please don't skin me.* The only force stronger than birds had been the Bump, for after she appealed to him, the staining birds vanished from her dreams. And oddly, now that the Bump had hatched into Dion, he cried like a bird. High-pitched. *Skree, skree.* A sea bird.

She couldn't tell about Dion and was no longer sure of his magic, but Morgan held hope as she pedalled hard against the wind on the black streets, home from the Dairy Queen... and the birds watched balefully from the back of her mind.

THREE

November

Louise was curled on the bed, as she'd lain there weeks before, following her fight with Gavin. She felt frail and translucent. Gavin came in to talk, but his touch sickened her, left her numb. She had visions of neighbours hovering like harpies around their house. *This isn't me it's happening to. I'm not here, it's not my life.* Her jaws ached from clenching her teeth as she slept at night.

Dion's crib was in their room. *Skree, skree.* She shut her eyes so hard against the sound that bolts of scarlet burst into the black. His cry was foreign and weak, mewling. Nobody used that word, but there it was, spelled in copperplate script inside Louise's head: mewling.

She had been pumping her breasts, giving him her own milk by bottle. Dion couldn't suck properly: his head lolled, his mouth couldn't latch onto her, his eyes couldn't focus on her. Blessed Dion. St. Francis would have loved him, carried him in his woolly brown sleeves like a pink kitten, laid him down with ocelots and lambs and little sparrows.

It was Louise's nature to regard, for several weeks, all of her babies as exotic, barely human creatures of sweet smell, and she existed with them in a slightly mystical other reality—caused no doubt by hormones, exhaustion, and adjustment to the exchange from within to without—which kept herself and child aloof for that period. Gradually, as their prebirth qualities disappeared, there emerged a proper baby, and the magic would sigh its way out of the house. Dion lingered with Louise in that early union, but unhappiness threatened to suffocate their love, and pity was at risk.

Louise had walked to the drugstore the night of Dion's birth as one bewitched, fooled first by her reconciliation with Gavin and then by a bright moon in clear black air. Then, right in front of her, that poor old man died. Folded down like a fan, soft and noiseless. But she saw blood. Instead of her water, impossible blood. She watched it, thinking at first the old man was injured by some force she'd failed to notice, and it was his life oozing away into little tide pools around her feet.

"You're a lucky woman, Mrs. Protheroe," they told her at the hospital. "We almost lost you both."

Lost. A word her mother would use. *Where'd you lose that friend of yours, Mother,* Louise always wanted to say, *in the sock drawer? Say it. Died. They died, are dead. They are completely and utterly dead.*

But lost, too, maybe. If Dion had died, she might be forever looking for him, signs of him, wondering if he was caught in a place where he could think about her, maybe see her. Myrtle Murray certainly lost her baby, not knowing where he would go. Lost her baby and didn't know where to find him, like sheep. Did she look for him anytime? Did she ever tell Edmund? Gavin lost his parents—not even Louise knew exactly where.

Dion was lost in spite of what they claimed. What he might

have been was lost for sure. Part of his mind was gone forever, so parts of his body could never catch up.

Gavin's good friend, Roland O'Grady, knew of a man in Florida who had a pathological fear of alligators. Roland told Louise and Gavin this at their dinner table, as he did most of his stories, in a voice whose authority easily carried across large rooms and with a flourish of hands and large gestures. He said that the man was eventually killed by being dragged into a swamp, rolled and drowned and chewed on. Truth was, according to Roland, the man succumbed to his fears, and this horrible end was his own doing.

Louise argued that the man had a premonition, and that was the foundation of the fear. Although she didn't support Roland's theory, it worried her and set a seed of caution within: just in case, Louise, don't go around imagining awful things or even dreaming them with much potency. Rachael would call it tempting the gods.

Louise had a little thought, which she immediately repressed, that by carrying a vision since childhood and fearing it, she herself had turned Dion into a Blue Baby, at least at his birth. Roland would believe.

As she lay hunched and miserable, eyes squeezed shut and head pounding, she knew she should get up right away and start dinner. She believed herself to be something like the person Rachael saw, a practical, sensible woman who could handle anything. Anything. And better than most people, including the rest of her family. This distress would pass. It had to.

Louise found herself unable to tell her daughters what had happened the night of Dion's birth. It wasn't that she didn't try to explain, but she choked on the words, and what came out was altered. In fact, she believed she'd said what she intended. Gavin traditionally looked to Louise as the communicator in the family, so if he wondered at her choice of phrase, he didn't contest it. He figured she knew what she was saying.

What this actually meant was the twins thought that Dion was sick. And sick people get better, so everything would soon be back to the way it was. Morgan knew something was weird about Dion, but he always was a mystery, so she had faith. Gale was not going to let anything hurt her mother, and if Louise wanted Dion to be okay, then he was, and when certain neighbours flashed their phony smiles at Gale and asked nosey questions, well, she didn't give them any satisfaction. As for Celia, she did up her long, dark hair and studied herself in the mirror as she cradled Dion in various maternal positions. She patiently awaited the day he would perform brilliant baby antics, telling her friends that the difficult birth had delayed some things, and see what she'd bought for her cute little brother.

And Dion *was* cute. His red-gold hair was starting to curl, as Myrtle Murray had predicted. And his round face was enigmatic, still as a picture and glowing. His eyes remained a startling purple-blue, refusing to convert to their own colour as his sisters' had, and were framed by long golden lashes. He didn't focus on anything but lay quiet and mostly unresponsive, mouth slack. "Sometimes," Louise told Gavin, "it feels like I've given birth to a delphinium."

Gavin would never say so, but he grieved almost constantly for the partial loss of his son, who would face struggles and taunts and a limited life. The pain intensified Gavin's love, and he regretted he'd once wished Dion had never happened. He bore another burden of guilt, for he held himself responsible for Louise's suffering. Although he refused to believe that she could easily have died, he knew there had been too many babies for her, and he should have made sure they quit. But if they had, there would be no Dion.

Gavin held what he considered to be a silly notion that

somewhere, heaven, maybe, there were children waiting to be born to certain parents, little lineups eternally ready for the moment of conception. This image must have come from some religious training in his distant past, for he couldn't explain it and would hardly admit to himself he thought it. When Gavin was growing up, he never imagined one day he would be surrounded by six of his own children. If a fortune teller had predicted this, he'd have demanded a refund, more easily believing he was destined for a stint in jail, bad luck in a foreign land, or an early death. His was not a life of much hope, and when ambition glimmered in his nineteenth year, he put it away to make room for Louise and kept it hidden as a faint light at the bottom of a long flight of stairs.

For ambition was not necessary for his survival, but Louise was. Louise anchored him and loved him in a way that seemed impossible to the phantom voice of his childhood, and when she still wanted him after their first big fight, he was in a state of glory.

What a strong young man he seemed to Louise's parents, big and capable, looking after his family so well, such a quiet man. And the phantom voice, curled and poorly hidden, hissed contemptuously to Gavin that nothing would ever go right for him; he was no good and came from no good and never would amount to a hill of beans; he would never live in a normal family, and Dion just proved it.

Whenever the voice got too loud, Gavin said to it, *Shut up.* Out of everything he'd tried, that was the most effective. Over the years, his friend Roland discussed with him Gestalt and Jungian dream therapy and poisonous relationships. Roland was a self-made analyst. His real job involved counting train cars. He'd known Gavin a long time, had even tried his hand at seducing Louise once before Gavin married her. Roland still had a crush on Louise and kept telling her so, but always when

Gavin was around to hear. Only once did these affections make her mad, and that was when he brought one of his girlfriends, an insipid straw-haired vegetarian, to dinner and, while mooning over her, said, "You and Louise are so similar, like you share some ancestry—you have the same kind of beauty." Louise smiled tightly and ran upstairs as soon as she could to put on more makeup.

Roland was always falling in love. He had a couple of sons, one of whom he visited somewhere in the interior of British Columbia, but the other boy had moved away with his mother years earlier and showed no interest in knowing his father. Roland had never married, although he came close a few times. He would save himself by suffering a raging depression, where he would hole up in his apartment every day after work for a few weeks, refusing to talk to friends and moping around drinking tequila and writing bad poetry. Sometimes, he'd invite a woman to join him. There always seemed to be an extra one somewhere who found him irresistible. He was a little worn around the edges, but his hair was thick and long, his face only got more interesting over the years, and women always felt he was deeply fascinated by their minds. If his current fiancée didn't find out about the other women, the fit of melancholy was enough to scare her off.

Roland and his pop psychology were an integral part of Protheroe household history. The girls grew up with him appearing at their door at odd times, sometimes not too sober, occasionally with a woman or just looking woebegone, but usually at mealtimes, ready for a long visit. He was about the only person who could get away with that. Louise had inherited Rachael's stern reaction to those who didn't know their manners and used various tactics to get people to leave. Gavin wouldn't have known the difference. If Roland wanted to visit whenever it was fine by him, and if he was busy, then Roland pitched in.

As Louise lay upstairs that day, Gale answered the door. "Come in, Your Flakiness," she said. Roland gave her a polite, one-armed hug.

"Still working out, I see," he said and handed her a big bag.

"Get serious! You didn't actually bring dinner with you, Your Rolandness? Hey, Mother Louise, haul yourself out of bed; Roland's here with deep-fried dead chickens and coleslaw."

Gavin went up to get her. It took fifteen minutes, but Louise came downstairs. She'd lost a lot of weight since the delivery, and the skin of her face looked stretched and drawn, her neck too thin. She'd remembered to brush her hair, but it was dry and breaking, and her lips were faded.

"Hi, dollface, you look beautiful," Roland said, kissing her.

Gavin looked at his friend. "When're you getting a wife?"

"Marrying is against my religion. You know that."

THE GIRLS HAD SCATTERED after dinner, and Louise heard bits of them reaching otherworldy from various parts of the house. The daughters she couldn't identify by voice, she attempted to locate by some hidden sense—testing, briefly, whether this was in her power as a mother. Her hand rested on the handle of the fridge. She tried to remember what was said to them before they left, about homework or if Dion should cry or piano practice or brushing teeth.

She looked at her hand, puzzled. Coffee beans.

The bag was fat and cold, too heavy. The open refrigerator cast an extra layer of light over her bare feet, revealing them as widened and crude, too old to be casually displayed like this. She felt indecent as if she'd appeared partially dressed—in a corset, maybe, bulges squishing out for the company to see.

Somehow, as she put the beans on the counter and plugged in the kettle, a china cup got in her way: Gale's baby cup, with Beatrix Potter rabbits in bonnets and jackets. The only reason Louise had taken it from the shelf was that there were hardly any clean dishes. She heard her breath suck in as the cup left the counter and began its slow fall toward linoleum. She felt almost weightless and could do nothing but reach out a clumsy arm that followed the arc of the cup's descent, cream-coloured bone china with picnicking rabbits spinning gently to the floor. It bounced. Once. And lay there, impossibly intact.

Gavin bent over from his chair and handed the cup to his wife. He watched her blow off germs, then hide it at the very back of the cupboard. The kettle steamed and began to shriek. Louise leaned against the stove, rubbing her face with the heel of one hand and holding an idle coffee grinder in the other. Gavin pushed aside plates and gooey cardboard to make room for his elbows. He sighed loudly.

Louise looked up at him. Red blotched her cheek where she'd kneaded it, and her eyes were bright and wet-lidded from fatigue.

She said, "I heard that."

"You didn't hear a damned thing." But Roland was already at her side, and Louise allowed him to take the grinder from her. He set mugs and a sugar bowl on the counter with the hand not occupied with pulverizing beans. Louise couldn't tell what was expected of her—if she should pretend to help him, sit with Gavin at the filthy table, or disappear upstairs because she looked like shit.

Roland brushed her upper arm gently with his knuckles, up and down. The mugs had been filled. She said to Roland, "I look like shit."

He studied her a moment carefully. Louise was afraid he might scent a whiff of madness on her, and would understand that she was not able to make sense of her own kitchen.

But he said, "You're lovely. Sit down and visit before the little villain wakes up."

She watched Gavin as she sipped her coffee, expecting him to shoot her a private look, reproachful or critical. When their eyes finally met, he immediately turned back to Roland and sprawled out his legs, leaving no room for her own.

She tucked a foot, Japanese-style, beneath her and wrapped the other around the chair. The leg she sat on began to cramp, and the cramp grew satisfyingly to pins and needles until, as she listened to Roland, it finally went numb.

"Hell," said Gavin, "We saw your Uncle Pete in action last winter, didn't we, Louise? Downtown, praising the Lord and handing out tracts. Don't think he even recognized us. He was all ablaze, glowed like the damned Pope."

"He was very polite," said Louise firmly. She had liked Pete, whom they'd met at a wedding. A courteous, handsome man in his seventies whose religious and political advice tended to wear people down. He drove two hours into the city most weekends for his mission work.

"I was there Wednesday," continued Roland. "Ten miles down that hilly grid in the kind of wind that turns your nuts to brass. Landed in at one in the afternoon, and there's Pete, all hunched over in a corner scowling at his Bible, and Auntie Anne and the neighbour lady sitting at the kitchen table sucking back tumblers of whisky and water. Turns out that old Zacharias character died, so they'd all been at prayers in the morning. Uncle Pete says Zacharias was quite the mechanic. Did the combine for him a couple of summers ago, worked cheap. So, I guess Pete was off on the swather already, and Anne gives Zacharias a whisky before he gets going on the combine. Pete looks up at me, all mournful, and says, 'I went off and did the swatting for the day, and when I went to use that combine the next week, it fell apart right in the middle of the field.'"

Louise wondered how Pete viewed this wild nephew; if he loved Roland very much or cordoned him off as he did most of humanity in need of salvation.

Gavin said, "Guy at work's got a friend who used to be a monk but figured the monastery was too slack. Nobody's seen him for a year. I said, 'I bet he's a hermit now, like a holy man. He's probably out there somewhere, living in the bush or on the prairie, chanting to jackrabbits and Russian thistle.'"

This appealed to Louise. If the world altered to allow it, she'd build a hut shaped like a beehive, and the wind would blow off sea cliffs all around. She decided on the spells needed to ward away intruders. She would appear as the gnarled root of a shrub, a dried bunch of milkweed or heather, something inedible.

Celia stood beside her, Dion in her arms.

Louise tried to get up, but her right leg objected. She kicked Gavin with the left, and he moved out of her way. She managed to take the baby from her daughter and hobbled peg-legged around the kitchen, preparing a bottle. Dion breathed warm and soft from the curve of her arm, staring without commitment in whatever direction he was facing.

She counted her children. "Where's Gale?"

Celia answered. "Downstairs."

The other three, Morgan, Hazel, and Fay, cluttered the kitchen, looking for ice cream or some of those chocolate things she'd made.

"That was days ago. They're eaten." Maybe. Louise couldn't remember which chocolate things they meant.

She snuggled into a living room armchair with Dion and

placed the rubber nipple against his lips, coaxing them. He blinked into the lamp. His mouth soundlessly shaped *whoo, whoo.* Her breasts began to ache and harden. A ring of milk grew, soaking the shirt under Dion's head. *Whoo, whoo.* He clamped down on the bottle as if in response to his mother's need and began to suck.

She could hear Roland in the kitchen, explaining the critical aspects of poker dice, and then Fay's and Hazel's squeals as they ran up to their room to get pennies for betting. She almost switched Dion to her other breast but remembered and willed the milk to stop. It had to wait for the ridiculous pump and little plastic bags.

Sometimes, when Roland was between women, he and Gavin and Louise would stay up late, like kids at summer camp, playing rummy or poker. But even this familiar picture—along with everything else—appeared bent somehow.

"For godsake, Mom," yelled Gale, "turn down that awful music. We're trying to watch *Wheel of Fortune.*"

Applause welled from the television. Tthe wheel spun again. Morgan said, "Buy an I!" The wheel spun, *tickety-tick,* bankrupt—no, just past it. More applause.

Gale pulled a French notebook from her bag and conjugated verbs as she spun with the wheel, yelling out the right letter just in time.

Just in time, a battle formed. Down the alley behind the movie theatre, there was a loud scream. Gale ran toward the sound. Traffic noises faded, street lights dimmed. She could see a struggle. Three guys had her sister Morgan. Morgan's face was bleeding and bruised. No, it wasn't. They hadn't touched her yet. One held a knife. *You ugly bastard,* Gale screamed, *leave her alone!* She kicked the knife from his hand, heard the crack of bone.

Go away, little girl, taunted another.

Make me, you ugly prick! and she stomped his instep. *Run, Morgan!* she screamed.

Morgan ran. The third guy kicked hard behind Gale's knee —she was down. This was it.

Death came quickly. The funeral was large, emotional. Her mother hugged little bundled Dion. Gavin had all the guys from work, and everyone from Gale's school was there. Sean. Sean was crying, his long, strong hands covered in tears and snot. She loved him so much. She hadn't known until then that he really loved her.

Gale's eyes glistened as she got up from her homework to stretch. "I'm going for a bike ride."

"Yup," said Morgan, studying what Vanna White wore as she spun the Wheel of Fortune, a chic suit armoured in silver sequins. Celia would have something to say about that suit. "Win," she said to the little television woman with the newly permed hair and the crooked teeth. Morgan thought of her own fist clutched full of cash, how much she might need to buy a twin-engine. Or a small jet.

Louise called from the kitchen, "Gale, if you're going out anyhow, take Dion with you."

It was almost the middle of November, the air was dry and harsh, and there was still no snow. Gale remembered some winters that started in September and lasted until April and having to trick-or-treat through Halloween snowdrifts, dragging the twins in a toboggan behind.

This was a dreary day when evil whirlwinds sprang up from nowhere to funnel old leaves and dust and scraps of paper, dragging them down the street into Gale's face. She spat. The air had a bite, and she pulled up the hood of her bunny hug. Tangent's leash was tied to the handle of the baby carriage, and he trotted happily between Gale's feet, where she'd boot him, and the back wheels, where he'd jump back surprised each time he ran into them as if they'd only just appeared. Dion was in a knitted cap under a fat quilt, blinking at the bits of sky that burst between treetops.

He was very quiet, as Gale expected him to be. At home, he would often lie for hours, uncomplaining, in his crib or slouched in an infant seat with towels rolled up on either side of his head for support.

He never smiled.

Sometimes, when Tangent barked frantically, Dion would squeeze his eyes shut. He rarely cried, but once he started, it seemed he didn't know how to stop, and the strength and pitch of his sobs were awful. The Protheroes were very careful not to do anything to provoke him.

But rolling along the sidewalk, bouncing gently over the cracks, with Tangent's nails clicking on the pavement and Gale whistling softly between her teeth, he was content.

Gale usually walked Dion toward the west since the Weir's house was on the east side of their own. She couldn't stand that family. It was Gale who'd dubbed Curtis and Colin the Weird Boys, but to be fair, she thought, Curtis and Colin were made peculiar by accident—accidentally being born to those parents —so technically, they were innocent.

Thank heaven she hardly ever ran into Mister they-weren't-allowed-to-call-him-Larry Weir; it made her teeth hurt if she was forced to talk to him. Lots of people seemed to think he was really nice, but his voice was too gooey and smooth, so she figured he must be hiding something. "And how are you-oo?" he'd ask, all faggy-eyed under his glasses. *Nazi. Like he really cared.* Louise insisted that the girls be polite to them anyhow and had a fit if she thought they weren't. Gale couldn't figure out why her mother bothered.

Gale didn't mind walking Dion, even if she was freezing. She'd never done much babysitting for other families, preferring to rake leaves or shovel sidewalks for cash, but even so, she knew he wasn't quite right. He was a little guy still; maybe he'd grow out of it. She saw how her mom looked sometimes when Dion was crying, when he really got wound up, and nobody could comfort him. Louise would put on the stereo full-blast or start up the vacuum cleaner and work furiously for half an hour with every muscle in her face contracted. The noise would finally break the inertia of his wailing, but it took longer for Louise's face to get back to normal. Sometimes until the next day.

They were almost at the park where she liked to take Tangent for a run. Gale crossed the street quickly to get into the shelter of thick conifers and out of the cold. It wasn't so safe here at night, but the huge black trees were comforting and deadened the wind. She turned the carriage off the main path and headed down a twisting walk, soft with pine needles, toward a bench she knew was around the corner. Someone was already there, a very elderly woman.

Sometimes, on their walks, she would meet up with people who liked to admire babies, and they would want to talk to her as they looked down at Dion and tell her all kinds of things about their children or their grandchildren. Gale wasn't usually very conversational, but she tried hard with them, especially if they were old. She really got a kick out of old people.

Even poor old Mrs. Murray, who came over about a million times when Louise was in the hospital, bringing casseroles, all guilty and saying she should have known, like it was her fault Louise had a bad time because she wasn't warned by Mrs. Murray's stupid psychic dreams. But Gale respected her for the way she loved Dion and said what a happy baby he was, although he had never smiled once since he was born. Gale figured he'd smiled lots of times when he was the Bump, but somehow, getting born had made him forget how. She knew how he felt.

The woman on the bench was definitely older than Mrs. Murray. Gale wondered how this one had managed to walk herself to the park. She looked like she could hardly sit there without the wind tipping her over. Gale knew all about osteo-porosis; it was drummed into them enough at school. This lady had it, for sure—she was curled right over like a wrinkled bean, and the hand on her cane was knobby and twisted. She wore a churchy blue hat with a little veil that didn't cover anything and a huge hatpin stuck through it, and her coat was blue. Her shoes were the chunky black kind with little holes all over, and although her legs were like sticks, her feet puffed over the tops of the shoes. They looked very uncomfortable.

Gale smiled at her dutifully. "Do you mind if I sit here?"

The woman patted the bench beside her, and Gale plunked down. "Is this your baby, dear?"

"My brother, Dion. I'm fifteen."

She leaned over the carriage, and Gale thought she had never in her life seen so many lines in a face, like an African drought on skin. The woman put her crooked hand on Dion's cap. He was still staring at the sky. "God bless him. He's got the healing, you know."

"He's not sick."

"I know, dear. I mean, he's got the healing."

"Oh," said Gale. She liked the way elderly people said stuff like that. She was never sure if they were batty or really knew something, or only forgot to end their sentences.

"I'm fine. You go on now. You look like a girl in a hurry."

How'd she know that? Are all old ladies psychic? No, her grandmother wasn't.

"Nice to have met you," said Gale.

The woman laughed as if she could tell Gale had to work at being gracious, and Gale ran behind the carriage out of the park, back into the wind. It wasn't as bitter now, raging behind her, but she could hear a winter's howl at its back.

Almost home, and damn: Curtis and Colin.

"Hi, Gale."

"Hi, Gale."

"Can we see Dion?"

"Yeah, can we see Dion?"

"Please, just for a minute."

"Hi, Dion."

"Yeah, hi, Dion."

"Hey, Gale, is he still a retard?"

Gale grabbed the Weird by one ear and held on tight. "Who said that to you, you ugly little shitfaced idiot?"

"I was kidding. Let go, nobody said that to me, it was a joke, let go, I didn't mean it, let go."

"Yeah, let go, Gale, he didn't mean it."

Gale was shaking and said through her teeth, "You tell your mother Dion is not a retard, and you tell your father that Dion is not a retard, and don't ever show me your ugly little faces again."

Curtis and Colin ran for their front door, and Gale could hear them crying and calling as they went into their house. Then, Margo Weir loomed in her doorway, looking from her boys back to Gale, and Gale could feel that stare like a dentist's drill, and she thought, *oh, shit*. She kept walking very quickly, right past the Weirs' house and her house to the end of the block and around the corner, faster, and Tangent started barking. She'd forgotten to let him have a pee, but she kept going and knew the phone would be ringing at the Protheroe house, and Margo Weir would bitch away at Louise, and Louise would be all apologetic and mad at the Weirs but madder at Gale, and Gavin would be waiting to give Gale a lecture about her temper, and Louise would get depressed again.

Skree, skree.

"Not now. Shit. Please, Dion, please, not now."

An old guy heading up his walk called to her, "You'd better get that little feller home for some supper."

She nodded, her face on fire, barely able to hold back her own tears. Maybe if she got near heavy traffic, the noise would distract him, and he'd quit crying, but people would hear him first and talk to her, and she couldn't stand it.

They left a trail behind them as they went—remnants of

her curses, Dion's cries, Tangent's yips. Home was the last place Gale wanted to be.

"Luminous," said Hazel, looking out the window, "luminous luminosity."

"Looniness," said Fay. "Looniness looniosity."

"Dion is luminous when sleeping."

"Leon is duminous when sleeping."

"Here he comes with Gale."

"Cere he hums with Gale."

"No, he's coming up the walk right now with Gale."

"That's too long, I can't say it," said Fay.

GAVIN HEADED BACK to the shop, pushing his tool cart. Some days, it felt like a ton, drawers and shelves loaded, plus a few big cases. Some days, the cosmos got distracted and let a New York City architect design the library for a prairie campus—an award-winner who didn't understand a place where temperatures drop or rise sixty degrees in a day, where averages mean nothing. No money to fix it; just go in and fiddle.

Celia could be here soon. Less than a year, he hoped, unless she found the guts to do some crazy thing like audition for an acting program. He backed through the door, pulling the cart, shoved it against a wall, and unclipped his pouch and radio.

The others were already sitting, a dozen on his crew looking after valves, thermostats, any automated control on the grounds. They did the round table for twenty minutes, went over directives from on high, and dealt with the call list for middle-of-the-night rescues. He was at the bottom again. Louise couldn't handle it when he'd gone in last week. Neither could he. He told the guy on call about the second-floor fan, just in case.

At four-thirty, the rest blasted off, leaving him and Stan, who would visit with a doorstop if nobody else was listening. Gavin noticed Stan's hair, thick and curly, getting browner by the day, and briefly wondered about his own age-flecked beard.

"Hey, how went the libra—" Stan turned to adjust his dentures, and Gavin pretended not to look. Stan had got his teeth, the whole mess, yanked last summer. Took a week off to go fishing and lived on aspirin and whisky. He'd told them, "It hurt like a damn, but I learned something. There's lots of words just can't be said with gums." He righted himself and beamed, dead even top and bottom. "How went the library, boss?" Stan called them all boss, but Gavin was the real thing.

"She was a bitch, thanks for asking, but I think I've shut her up for a while."

"So what you got for me tomorrow?"

"4F-63 Agriculture. I want to do a room commission if the electric's done. If we can't get in, you've got the fume hood in Biology." Gavin zipped his jacket, pulled out a cigarillo, and stuck it in readiness behind his ear. He nodded. "'Night, Stan."

"Hey, boss, how's the runt making out?"

"Great. I'm training him so's he can take over your job in a couple of months."

Stan laughed. "Thanks for the warning."

Gavin fielded a lot of admiring insults over the size of his family. A hundred and some tradesmen he joked with over the year and another huge group of faculty and students would become friends with no names. He could easily count on his fingers those he knew anything personal about; the rest might cheat on their taxes or their wives or beat their kids. A false society; it didn't matter, he talked to them all.

He put up his collar and hunkered against the wind. Only Wednesday, and he was exhausted. He'd staggered downstairs that morning at six and found Louise passed out in the kitchen rocker, clutching Dion.

The wolf in his gut got him worried nobody was making dinner, and then he remembered Rachael had made one of her infrequent overnight visits. He cut through the Administration building on his way to the parking lot.

Gavin knew the university the way a probing doctor comes to know a body. He had been through every turn of its warm bowels, crossed forbidden lawns, met rats in crawl spaces, unlocked barely used doors. He'd seen buildings rot and given to lesser departments, others built and dedicated. Watched profs age with him. Knew some who ran from their day straight for the bar, some who came early to work. There were smarmy guys who never acknowledged him, but a few who loved to talk, like the timid Vet Med prof who slipped him literature on the Communist Party.

After fifteen years there, he knew lots about air balance, how rooms suck and breathe. He only wished he could adjust something to make life less miserable for the students who passed him head-bent and tense. Exam-time air quality. That would be a calling.

GAVIN'S MOTHER-IN-LAW sat beside him, eyes fixed out her side window, hands folded next to the purse in her lap. They were half-blinded by the sun, which blazed at the end of the highway, ready to slide below the horizon.

That time of year, when the days shrank, waiting for the snows to come, the sun set quickly, savagely. On dreary days, it merely faded as if by dimmer switch. Rachael loved this drive, the landscape patchy and dry, trampled by deer, burnished by cold wind.

She also loved it in spring, when the haze of sharp green turned to leaves and flocks of birds, and in full summer, the windshield sticky with a rain of bugs.

She loved it at night anytime. The car became a ship at sea inside the weather, navigating by stars that scattered like flour dust shaken from a pastry cloth. Gavin could show her Hydra and Taurus and Cassiopeia. And Gale swore that twice she saw a UFO over the farm, a dark shape too fast and low, blotting out the stars. *Well, you never know.*

Rachael smiled as she thought of Fay phoning her to come stay the night. "Gramma, is that you?"

"Yes, dear, is everything fine?"

"Prove it's you. Who's our dog, and what's he smell like?"

"He's got red hair, and his name is, oh dear, it starts with T.

And on bad days, he smells like dirty socks, but usually he's very clean for a dog."

"You pass the Alien test. Hazel said I had to make sure."

She will pretend they are driving forever, her soul carrying right on down the road long after they've made the turnoff.

She wished Dean Martin was still on television. He was probably a bit of a womanizer, mind, but he could certainly sing.

"I said, are you warm enough?" said Gavin.

"Oh, yes, thank you, just fine."

Gavin watched the sun vanish, leaving the horizon charged with amber, barely holding the darkening sky, thick with cloud.

He was glad of the darkness; it closed off the silent-picture monochrome of late fall in the prairie. A nether season, short-lived and sad, that waited, inert, before true winter arrived.

He thought with longing of his bike. Heavy, black and silver, it could carry him farther west ahead of the snows, through the mountains, until he reached the mossy land of ravens and otters; and when the cold caught up to him, he would take the sea coast south until he was past the cities and into the dustier terrain of brown-skinned people. Gavin lingered there until he laughed to himself, realizing the fading image of the Mexican girl he married was straight out of a spaghetti western. He lifted Louise onto the bike, and she rode behind him, pale as a wraith and black hair streaming. But when they arrived, the desert's scorch withered her and she disappeared along with the six eggs of their children.

He could hear Rachael humming quietly beside him. Gavin turned north automatically, toward the farm. The washboard gravel rattled them along the dusk. As he reached over to turn up the heat, his eye caught the shadowed flash of an old pickup truck decomposing back of a hill.

He got a whiff of onetime dust and old memory of cracked seat leather, and he is bouncing through a field, and the grass is high as the windows and brushes his arm. He stretches out a hand to grab the yellow heads, and they sting along his palm, leaving a burn. He tries to see over the grass, but there's only barbed-wire fence and a post once in a while. Beside him is a big black knobbed stick shift with numbers on the end of it and round black things that you can pull out from the dash. "Don't touch that, son." Pipe smoke. Bounce along.

Where the hell is he? The sun is hot.

Gavin is five years old. This is a true story, he reminded himself, but not real to him as his brothers were when he'd created them. He had read things and believed he possessed the authentic Celtic soul, the mystic shade that travels unaided at night. He believed there were secrets that came to him during those flights, which he sometimes remembered briefly, that were first revealed and then imprisoned in his psyche, there to protect him.

He is five years old, and it is very dark. In the dark, his eyes create their own light, and phosphorescent wisps flit around him. Sometimes, he hears sounds and voices outside his space, but he has learned to pay them no mind, to make himself silent because it's only worse when he doesn't. His atoms disassemble.

The only thing that matters is the light returning. The only thing to enter this space is the light, and he never knows if the light, like a night dream, brings good or evil.

He used to cry in there. He used to think about food.

That's how he first learned to go invisible, then to disassemble.

He is five years old, his name is Gavin Protheroe, and a

man came one time in the blaze of light and said, "Here he is." And he never went there again.

It is a true story, but mostly false. It has nothing to do with him, it has nothing to do with his family, and it is not permitted entrance anywhere. Louise and Roland know a bit about it. That's all.

One time, when he is ten, a couple wants to adopt him, but he says, "What about my brothers?" And they change their minds. Because he doesn't have any brothers, and he forgets that and opens his big mouth. Just as well. They are grubby in that place, and the man's orange-stained fingers are forever fixing things at the kitchen table, toasters and irons and electric frypans, and the woman is forever telling Gavin he's come from trash and should be grateful.

Trash. He isn't sure about the meaning of that. Way back when, in the other place, the other woman with the dark and light hugged him sometimes and put him away sometimes. He mostly forgets. And the grubby people feed him lots. "Look at him eat. He'll be putting us in the poorhouse." But they seem to like that he eats so much—bread and margarine, meatballs and gravy, hash, peas from a can. Good food. "You'll never amount to a hill of beans." He imagines it, spooned from a giant can of Libby's, ketchup on top.

"Here we are, Rachael, home at last and pitch-black. Did you forget to call Harold to turn on the lights?"

"I phoned him. You know Father." Rachael waited for Gavin to open her door and help her from the van. It was cold, and exhaust muted the glare from the headlights as Gavin walked her into the porch. He felt his way through the black into the living room, where he found Harold sitting in the dark in front of the television. A cryptic smile from out of a blue chiaroscuro.

"What's your temperature gauge say out there, Harold?"

"Fifty."

"Fifty, are you sure?"

"'Bout that. Alls I know is, it's damn cold."

"You bet it's cold. About minus-eight right now. Well, I brought your bride home for you—thought you might be missing her."

Harold laughed.

FOUR

December

Not good, not good. Morgan stuffed the math paper back into her book bag. This kept happening; she'd be doing a test or something, and it was like somebody was humming in her ear: everything would quit making sense, and then it would be time to hand in the test, and Morgan would be half-done. She wiggled her feet into her boots.

Jessica walked past, rammed the side door with her shoulder, and stood there, holding it open to the cold, looking at Morgan. Thirteen years old. But almost fourteen, as she told everyone. Morgan thought she looked great—she had one of those Sherpa-looking pointy wool caps, and her long hair fuzzed out from under it.

"Hey, Jess, wait up."

"Morgan."

"How's Greg? He still there?"

"Yeah, but what the hell do you care?"

"I'm just being nice."

"Right. You were supposed to come over last week—we have the social studies thing to do. Remember, retard? Who the hell's gonna make the map? I can't draw worth shit, and you're so neat and tidy."

"You don't need to make it sound like a crime. I can't help if I draw neat."

"You do everything neat, Morgan. You're such a little citizen."

"A what?"

"Citizen. What Greg calls them, people like you."

"Jess, do you like Greg?"

"Why shouldn't I?"

"Nothing. I like him."

"Greg's fun."

"He's kind of a weird dancer."

Jessica laughed. Morgan was thrilled—finally, this must have been the right thing to say. She couldn't stand it without Jessica, and if she couldn't go to her house, where could she go and not be treated like a little kid? *And anyhow*, Morgan told herself, *nothing actually happened that time. Nothing really, right? Greg picked me up and carried me around for a bit, but he was drunk; I knew that, and Jess knew that. Nothing happened. Why do I keep dreaming about him? It's like I love him, except he's old. Maybe he was like a hero one time, and he saved a kid and I remind him of her. But Carolanne kind of hates me. What did I do? I wasn't going to drink that beer. I bet Greg never carries Jess around like that. He'd be like her dad, really funny and nice and give her stuff and never make her do housework. Oops, except Jess does lots of that anyhow. Maybe Carolanne makes her work that hard. Jess even has to put bleach in the dishwater. Mom says Carolanne must have been really young when she had Jess. Maybe Celia's age. Sick. Celia would never ever let some guy put his penis in her.*

"So, you coming over or what?" said Jess. She grinned at Morgan and looked like the real Jessica from when they would sing down the street together or sit at bus stops pretending to speak foreign languages.

"Yup. *Spinoid eska yumyum*," replied Morgan.

"*Scalla goria*. Let's stop at the 7-11 first. Carolanne's home, we can't get into the cupboards."

CELIA TRIED to concentrate on the monologue she'd written, though she knew it well enough. Almost everyone around her paced and mumbled and stretched or wandered glassy-eyed doing voice warmups—*ooh eeh oh bubba bubba*. Instead, she searched, inconspicuously, she hoped, for Jason. He was the most compelling guy she'd seen at school, stocky and muscular, one of the few who had a life—played bass in a band and did clever, hip cartoons for the school paper. She'd already spotted his girlfriend, Lara. Platinum hair, almost shaved. Nose ring, good jeans, antique jewellery: she always looked fantastic. Celia wondered what girls like that did in the old days. Maybe moved to Paris. Or just got in trouble.

Then she heard Jason's laugh and carefully shuffled her papers before turning to look. He leaned one arm into the wall; the other held his rolled-up script. Their drama teacher, Mr. Hembly, beamed down at him and said something, then pointed to his watch.

Ryan was first. He was mostly good-looking, with an unfortunate tendency to blush. Celia was sure he had a crush on her —he always deepened his voice when they spoke. But Celia would make vague references to a university student she was dating, never lying, exactly, but putting up some smoke. It was Jason she really wanted to watch.

She had to admit Ryan was funny. He was doing a ridiculous cowboy routine. "Your Cheatin' Heart" played in the background, and he took big swigs from a Budweiser bottle filled with something Mr. Hembly stopped the show to take a hard look at. The class was cracking up, making so much noise they had to be settled so he could finish. Her dad would have said he was spreading it a bit thick. "Mitzie, Mitzie, don't tell me you're never comin' back, I'm beggin ya, I'm on my knees to ya." Everyone thought this was hilarious. "And the kids misses ya, they've been bleatin' all day down in the pen." *For crying out loud, bring on Jason.*

And they did. Celia was so mesmerized for the next five minutes that she barely heard an entire sentence. Jason called it an alternative performance, and Celia thought it revealed incredible depth of character. He used masks he'd made, primitive things decorated with feathers and nails, and he talked about music in a way Celia couldn't quite make sense of. It didn't matter—he was too hot all by himself.

When Celia's name was called, she slipped a Pre-Raphaelite circlet of copper wire—one Gavin had made for her late the night before—around her brow. Mr. Hembly turned off the lights, and the spot blazed. She stepped forward in a long, velvety gown and turned. Her classmates had become the murky silhouette of an audience, and she stared past them and focused on the space under the blinding spotlight.

"How is it . . ." Her voice was odd, disembodied. ". . . that I am here, but I see myself there in the water. So still." She became the dead Ophelia, watching her own corpse float in the stream, deeply regretting her decision.

The applause was a faint hum. She wasn't sure if she'd said everything.

Morgan and Jessica slid down the sidewalk around to the back door, and there was the Volkswagen, like a big toy left out in the snow.

"It's the other odd one," said Carolanne to Morgan when they went into the kitchen. She didn't sound too hostile, almost friendly.

Uncle Greg called hello from the next room, and Morgan's stomach twisted a bit when he appeared in the kitchen doorway. He stopped and stretched. Morgan could see a dark nipple and its tuft of hair poking out of his sleeveless undershirt.

"Hey, girls. School out already, or did you rebels make a break for it?"

He ruffled Jess's hair, then gave Morgan a punch in the shoulder on his way to the fridge. He pulled out a beer, opened it, and handed it to Carolanne before getting his own.

"Thanks, baby." Carolanne had her chair tipped back and one leg on the kitchen table. She held the beer by her fingertips, sipping carefully with pinky extended to preserve the fresh coat of polish on her nails.

She loves him. Look at her.

It was all so familiar and welcoming Morgan knew she must have been mistaken about that whole family—she'd been dead wrong to worry.

Jess had been spinning around the room, acting goofy and filling her face with nacho chips. "Want some, Greg?" Jess held the bag out to him.

"Always," said Greg. He took a few and left the room.

"You're really some little piece of work," hissed Carolanne. Morgan thought she was making a joke—she had to be. Some sort of joke she didn't quite get.

Jess scowled at her mother. "I wasn't doing anything. I just offered him a treat."

Carolanne straightened the chair and pulled her foot off the tabletop, but her heel caught the nail polish and knocked it to the floor. She looked over at Morgan like she wanted to spit at her, picked up the polish, and checked the glass for cracks.

"Get the fuck out of here, Jess, and take your cute little friend with you."

Morgan felt sick. "Sorry, Carolanne." *Why did she say that?* She had no idea what they were supposed to have done.

They wandered through the living room, but Greg was there with headphones on, so they went to Jess's room, where they spent a couple of hours making a map of the new Europe.

When they'd finished their work, they discovered Carolanne and Greg had gone out somewhere, so Morgan phoned home to say she would eat with Jessica. They found mushroom soup in the cupboard and put together buttery grilled cheese sandwiches. Old times, she loved it.

After a while, they heard the front door open. Greg came in alone. He threw his coat in a corner on the floor and rolled his eyes at them.

"I guess Carolanne wants some space." He grinned and opened the fridge. "Fine with me. It'll be more fun helping you two with KP duty."

Morgan couldn't see anything fun about cleaning.

But that night, she went home feeling pretty good. It was a riot doing dishes with Greg. And he told them about some girls he knew in high school and how his uncle taught ballroom dancing. Treated them like they had brains in their heads, not as if they were children.

FIVE

January

$\mathcal{L}$ ouise's sentence lasted four months. This anguish had her trapped—she functioned in a torpor, unmoved to tears or real anger.

She puzzled at how each of the years spent with babies had tumbled in hot pursuit one after the next, leaving her almost forty and the last, astonishingly, almost leaving her dead.

Louise remained at the whim of waking dreams, dreams to be endured and analyzed, repeated over and over. She dreamed of herself. Why wouldn't they say it, Gavin and the girls, her mother and father, that she almost died? Almost lost. But she was lost. Gone somewhere, a small shift from where she was supposed to be, but gone nonetheless. Nobody welcomes death but saints and martyrs and heroes and those in unbearable pain. Louise resented rubbing shoulders with such exalted company.

It seemed she had survived some bizarre test but was left with guilt that she suffered more for herself than for her son.

Louise had the highest marks in her graduating class: higher than shrimpy Alvin Harris, who became a dentist, and higher than her clever friend Edwina, with whom she was once so close they couldn't imagine life without the other.

She dreamed of what might have been but couldn't delete any of her children from those scenarios—there they all were, no matter what. Maybe if Gavin had had lots of money, maybe then she would have had her babies and gone to university, and she'd be teaching somewhere, or have a medical degree, or do social work. Like being thirteen again, vocational and IQ tests: *Who am I and where should I go?* Impossible now. The thief of years had been and gone.

She dramatized visits with Edwina, who had loved her so much. Edwina left for university in Toronto on a science scholarship, and for a year or so, they wrote on a weekly basis and phoned one another often. They used to speak in that intimate way people do who have shared everything and witnessed together their adolescence, in half-sentences, private references.

It took ages before Louise finally understood that she had been dismissed from Edwina's life as someone who wasn't worth the effort, someone who stayed at home and had babies. Edwina made one visit when she came back to help her parents prepare for their move to the coast. It was shortly after Celia was born. She took one look at Louise's crummy furniture and her solid, quiet husband and said to Louise that she must have married Gavin because he was a good lover. Conspiratorially. They laughed, Louise feeling like a betrayer. Edwina tossed her fine blonde hair and oohed over tiny Celia, "She's perfect, like a little Michelangelo drawing," and presented her with an expensive, too-small white dress, which Celia wore once. That was the last Louise saw of Edwina.

She thought of Gavin roaring into the farmyard on his BMW bike that first time when she was seventeen, how alarmed Rachael and Harold were at the sight of him in old jeans and fringed suede, their relief when he took off the helmet, and they saw auburn hair cropped short as always. He had marvellous manners and knew his way around motors, which immediately bonded him to Harold.

She remembered Harold and Gavin in the shop, stooped over some problem on the bench, Rachael at the kitchen window, and how she'd waited by the west flower bed, wearing a new car coat and two layers of mascara, worried Gavin would get grease on him and leave a mark on her, or they'd be late for their first movie.

He stood over six feet, but there was a roundness to his shoulders as if he were trying to subdue his big frame so he wouldn't intimidate, different from the guys she'd known at school who matched him for size. They wore boots that made them taller and walked with their shoulders thrown back, and their feet met the earth with a force.

Louise had watched Gavin talking with the boys at the sand hills, could see his face brighten at something and his hands and arms get going, but the conversations seemed to fade, leaving him looking puzzled. Some of the girls told her he was hard to talk to or was boring or said things they didn't get, which made her wonder. The night he finally found her, Louise saw first his worried brown eyes, then a faint scar cutting one brow, disrupting the thick line. They talked easily, comfortably, and smiled together. She liked the way he searched her face and paid attention to anything she did or said, aware of her tiniest gestures, and he had stood when she got up to stretch.

She'd wanted to touch him. But the distance she kept was not because of Rachael's lectures on "boys know what kind of girl," it was Gavin's own fragility she had sensed.

He'd pulled a thin metal box from his jacket, lit one of his tiny cigars, and said, "You are a rare woman., Louise

Timmons," warming her at being called a woman. She used to think high marks would be her ticket out of there, away from marrying a farmer. Finally, though she knew Gavin Protheroe wasn't exactly an intellectual or didn't seem especially ambitious, she'd let her loins be the final judge.

So, Louise deeply regretted that little giggle with Edwina at Gavin's expense. In this pageant, she told Edwina what kind of person Gavin was, how he would prove to weather Louise's moods so well and love their babies and wash out the fridge and never look at another woman, how he said things to Louise in their embraces that put her on fire, how he treated her used body as the most erotic thing on earth.

In her reveries, Louise was part of another pageant where she visited with the image of a man, one not much older than herself but whose addictions degenerated his body. The man is Wilbur Hancock on the night of Dion's birth. Like a ghost in an old manor house, Louise revisits the scene. The poor man, his simple face crazy and addicted. How had they let him into the store with a dog? He smiled at her pregnancy; then he crumpled, he died. Did the Bump know at that instant that he might be taking the same journey as Wilbur? Did he smile back at that lonely man, one innocent to the other? Did they shrug at the caprices of life as they headed off, the Bump on an exhilarating ride to birth where death was equally possible? In Louise's version, she bestowed death to Wilbur as a great release, and he gave up his ghost with grace and ease. In Louise's version. Wilbur said happily, "Whoops, here I go."

Dion was changing. Even through her shadowed perception, Louise was able to see it. But she knew her terms of joy were unique for this baby who couldn't compete with the brilliant infant manoeuvres of his sisters. A couple of months after he lost his lovely newborn smell, his piercing cry was gradually replaced by a more subdued wail, and she counted it a small blessing. And another blessing when his purple blue eyes at long last showed signs of noticing his family, and again when his tiny neck held up the round golden head on its own.

Louise didn't notice when the grip of her torment began to lessen,when she was gradually carried away from its centre, on waves lapping out then back toward the pain, but out a little farther each time. One day, it was finally behind her. She began to feel herself bordering on sanity in the mornings when she woke, and some days achieved it. The memory of pain transformed her. It was an altered sanity, where things remained ambiguous.

Roland O'Grady had no plan—he liked to think of himself as an instinctive man, a man of the heart. He loved Louise, and it pained him to think she might be giving up. Her hair had a scratchy look, and the weight she'd lost didn't suit her, made the skin loose around her face and neck, and gave her mouth that stern appearance that sometimes fixed itself on older women. He always thought of her as well-rounded and blooming and often warned Gavin, "Watch that wife, Gav. Lots of men go for the fecund types."

Don't get old on me, lovely Louise; you're younger than I am, but if I saw you today for the first time, I would walk right by and not think of those green eyes or how I'd love to cuddle my face in your breasts.

Roland went that day to woo her somehow. He had phoned, and said, "I got laid off for a month and need a pal to celebrate with, you up to it?"

He put his head in the front door. "Louise?"

And there she was. Tired and smiling in one of Gavin's old shirts and a pair of jeans.

"You're still the most beautiful woman I know."

Coming from him, Louise could almost believe it. Roland meant everything he said, and she suspected he made many declarations to women, all of them true.

They sat side by side on the old couch, drinking wine and talking easily for a while, with Roland's arm around her. If her whole family had walked in at that moment, no one would have thought anything of it. Roland was one of them, and he and Louise often sat together like buddies. Louise figured Roland would find himself a younger wife when he was about fifty, when the wind was knocked out of him a bit and he needed a place to put up his feet for a few decades with somebody who could keep ahead of him.

He gave her a big hug, as he often did, but held her a little longer than usual, stroked her hair, folded it back and kissed her neck. Louise laughed and pulled away.

Since her world became changed, most events were of one intensity. Here was Roland, always concerned, next to Gavin, her closest friend. She trusted his face, puckish and worn. Louise was suddenly aware of the mischievous Roland, the one who could make a woman feel pretty good. She wondered what it would be like to have him inside her; suspected it might be weird and probably disappointing. This thought was natural flotsam in that foggy conscience, a little flitting banner, *thou shalt not.*

"Are you trying to cheer me up, Roland?"

"Whatever it takes."

"Don't worry about me; I feel almost human these days. Anyhow, it wouldn't have worked. I'm so moral it makes me crazy. I'm even moral in my sleep. You know, the most erotic thing I ever experienced in a dream was to slow dance with John Candy. I got horny with a comedian I'd never met. I know he's big and extremely sweet, but I thought people were supposed to let all kinds of things into their dreams."

"Maybe you take your dreams too seriously, and they know it."

"We danced in the kitchen."

"Kitchens are very sexy places."

"My kitchen?"

"Your kitchen is usually a mess, but a nurturing mess, from which rise miracles—fresh bread and chocolate cake and unusual spicy things; I like hanging around there. Don't tell me it makes me feel like a little boy again, my mother was no cook, believe me—she grew up in the back of a country store and learned to fix two-course canned dinners. Except you do have that hideous old stuffed rocker in there."

"I love that rocker."

"Exactly. Comfort. Louise, you know you are one of the most gorgeous women in the world, don't you? Not like a scrawny, souped-up fashion statement, more like something a guy craves when he's cold or sad. You would not believe how envious I was when Gavin married you—he was smart, went straight for quality. And you had this sharp tongue, not nasty, just cut to the meat of things, an épée conversationalist. Even when you were just out of high school."

"I didn't really know you then. I figured you were addicted to girls, any girl, and that's why you made the big move on me."

"Sorry. It was stupid, and Gavin would have killed me if he found out."

"Gavin knew."

"He did not."

"Give the man some credit."

"Here I thought I've been harbouring a dark secret all these years."

"Don't worry, Roland, I'm sure you've got lots more to harbour." Louise ignored the sting she felt, knowing she'd always been a little possessive of this man. She filled Roland's glass with wine, and he downed half of it. She'd barely touched her own. This was the extent of her own wickedness, drinking in the afternoon and while nursing, which—she thought dryly —was a generous definition of what she did for Dion.

What impressed Louise most about Roland's affection was his épée comment. It was a trait she couldn't see in either of her parents, certainly not in Rachael, who emulated her biblical namesake. Maybe it was Bridget. She must have had something reckless in her and strong, a young woman travelling alone halfway across the world. God, worse than anything Louise had had to face. "Maybe it came from Bridget. The sharp tongue, if it's true."

Roland doesn't mind this leap. "Makes sense, she was Irish. Predominant gene."

"There's not even a picture. There must have been something, courting letters or a wedding photograph. Wouldn't surprise me if my grandfather burned them all or some housekeeper at the farm threw them out. It's a crime."

"I don't know. Those portraits of my grandparents are all pretty awful, everybody stuck in oval frames looking depressed and put upon."

"Like me."

"You look a whole lot better than you did."

"I do?"

"Cut it out, Louise, it isn't healthy."

She emptied the bottle into Roland's glass. Louise loved these mildly drunken talks, especially when she was on the lucid end of them.

And that night, when the twins were doing the dishes, and Gale was walking Dion, Louise said she was tired. Gavin followed her upstairs. The world was starting to come back into focus.

HAROLD GRUMBLED CONTENTEDLY and settled himself deeper into the armchair. Rachael had fixed a pan of steaming water and salts for him, where his toes now wiggled like fat white babies. His feet had always been tender. They weren't yet married, Rachael remembered, the first time she sat him down and removed his shoes and socks. She had blushed, and her hands were tentative as she rolled up the cuffs of his trousers and carefully slid his puffy feet into the water.

She did this often for Harold at the end of the long days during farming seasons and in winter months when he'd haul grain or come in after fixing the odd thing in the dead cold of his dad's blacksmith shop. He'd sit in an earlier version of the same overstuffed chair in its spot next to the north window and across from the television. And he'd holler, "Is Red Skelton on yet, Rachael? Check the set for me, woman! Leave those dishes and get your fanny on out here before I miss my show."

She had no problem taking orders from her husband. Harold was always good-natured about being the boss. Rachael never thought she'd traded one indentured position for another; the duties of her new life were tempered by love and a fierce devotion to Harold.

Barely twenty years into their marriage, Harold's reason started to slip around. For a long time, she covered for him whenever she could, partly from shame and partly in the belief he would somehow recover from this nameless condition that sapped his mental strength. He was supposed to take care of her until death did them part. It was never agreed that she might have to figure things out and handle all the money and make arrangements with the man who rented their fields. Rachael had watched Louise begin directing her father and reluctantly copied some of Louise's techniques as she came to understand there were times she simply had to learn to put her foot down.

She looked again at Harold. He'd fallen asleep in the big chair, the remote control in his hand. She sighed, pulled the swollen feet out of the pan, dried them as he slept, and then tucked a blanket around his legs.

It seemed there was always work, though after seeing Louise with that brood of hers, Rachael could no longer imagine how she and Mama used to keep so powerfully busy with only Rachael's father to care of, him with the aches and pains and constant criticisms. "Lord knows she's no beauty, Mother. Good thing she's a working girl."

Girl! Why couldn't they see me as I was then—thirty years old—why, most of the gals from Normal School were married ten years at that age. They should have taken a look at themselves, those awful people—they could have been grandparents by then instead of jailers. Honour thy mother and father, my foot. But who else would have looked after them, I'd like to know, or possibly know how to do everything, and who on the Lord's green earth would have tolerated Father's temper tantrums? "He's an old man, Rachael, don't go on about him so." The old sod. Used to be Mama's excuse for him was his job at the mill, and then it was swollen joints and old age. And she was no better. How did I let it happen? At my age, caring for them like they were helpless kittens, Mama, the Queen of Sheba herself, with the vicious mouth, shrieking, "God sees you, Rachael. He sees what a bad child you are!"?

The bad child kneels in a corner and recites the Seven Deadly Sins, most of which she is accused of committing regularly. Pride, Covetousness, Lust, Anger, Gluttony, Envy, and Sloth. She is allowed to embroider the Seven Gifts, said to be infused into the soul upon baptism. Wisdom, Understanding, Counsel, Fortitude, Knowledge, Piety, and Fear of the Lord. Rachael sews them all into a sampler, which is framed and hung on her bedroom wall to the right of the fumed oak dresser.

And there she sees them every day of her life, and prays for forgiveness and the strength to commit these virtues to her black little heart. Little Rachael, long-nosed, doe-eyed, with her mother's narrow lips and her father's stubbornness.

Rachael has a cat, an outside cat, of course, because her mother can't abide an animal in the house—"This isn't a barn!" —a tortoiseshell with a white face and white paws named Please Sir, from *Oliver Twist*, a book she'd cried over many times. Beautiful Nancy, made blind by the cruel blows of her husband; brave, starving Oliver with his good heart, "Please, sir, I want some more." Little Rachael trudges through ordeal after ordeal at his side, protecting him, suffering with him, encouraging him.

She yearns to be a Dickens character and believes, a belief almost beyond hope, that there will be an earthly reward for her. It is not the beatings—many children she knew got them. Punishment is her parents' right, and she sometimes is a wicked child, certainly. It is that she never can do enough good deeds, enough work, never enough of her duty to suit her parents.

Rachael grew up with the housework and, eventually, her schoolchildren to think about, finally even had Harold Timmons on the sly. She began to see her parents differently as they aged until, from her mind's angle, it was like she stood atop a ladder looking way down at their heads, at the wispy hairs on her mother's pink scalp, and from that vantage, her father's body seemed dwarfed and misshapen. He had lain in bed with aching joints for company, crooked and bent, his horrible temper reduced to impotent curses. And she'd cried when he died and prayed fervently for forgiveness because they were tears of relief and thanks. Her mother was to be pitied then, so lonely, ruling alone, ruling nothing.

When Mama lay in her own last bed rest, widowed and old,

she cried not for her husband, who went the year before, but for the little blue baby. Invisible winds eroded her gradually so that every day, as Rachael carried up the breakfast, she saw a bit more of her mother had disappeared. There was barely a hair left on her head, and she wore a little dust cap. One arm was black, completely black from bruising during the fall that broke her hip, and she was dead white. Her mouth was open, and her teeth weren't in. Rachael said to herself, *She looks terrible, just terrible, so shrunken and faded. Like an old flower.* In the end, she was completely bald and had no anger or crossness left in her, only the simple requests of an old woman who knows she is dying and anything she might have done in this world is done. "Rachael, bring my ointment, bring a hot water bottle, another quilt, beef tea with biscuits. What did I hear you say down there? Who's Harold? Who's that on the phone, and don't tell me it's nobody. Really, Rachael, at your age, snickering on the telephone, don't think I can't hear you up here. Giggling like a shameless little girl."

And Rachael trudged back up the stairs, the waxed fir boards creaking under her slippers, tray in hand, covered in linen cloth embroidered with a small spray of bluebells and lily of the valley, done in lazy daisy stitch when she was ten or eleven, with little French knots in silk to make the buds. She used to sew her pain and troubles away in all these household linens. She stitched and thought of anything she pleased, although she knew God was right there inside her head, watching. She put a prayer in every complete flower, which was sometimes tricky when the design was such that some were partly hidden and some were bunched all together, but she gave them a Hail Mary anyhow. And if she was outside at the garden swing, Please Sir would come and rub his lovely dark russet flank against her legs, and if her parents were safely out of sight, then he might hop onto her lap and purr to beat the band. In three decades, she dragged herself up and down those stairs more times than she cared to know. And one summer, she noticed Harold Timmons giving her the eye at the store. When he asked what days she usually did the shopping, Rachael wondered at herself for telling him. She found him waiting there, after that, almost every week.

And September came. The grocer filled her order—to which Rachael added walnuts, maraschino cherries, and dates to be soaked in brandy for Christmas cake—had wrapped it all in brown paper and was tying it with string from the roll at the end of the counter. Harold crept up beside her and whispered, "Rachael, I could take you home in my pocket."

She'd jumped and tried to frown as she said, "Really. Of all the silly things."

Harold had piercing blue eyes and a rocky sense of humour that left her blushing deep and covering her mouth. He seemed a little unread, but that was common enough around there and didn't interfere with husband qualifications. What finally convinced her was Harold had no temper to speak of.

He asked her hand that winter. "Rachael, I have a tidy house and a farm to share. That's about the size of it. And I swear to look after you until death do us part, and if I ever raise a hand to you, well, God can strike me down." *Heavens,* thought Rachael, *that's a lot of promise.*

In those last days, Mama had drifted in and out of sleep. Rachael called for the priest, and Mama complained about the smell of pipe smoke on his breath. Then Rachael told her that she was going to marry Harold Timmons. Mama said, "Oh, dear," and died soon after.

Rachael took easily to her new home, and Harold was pleased to see a woman do her job right. True to his promise, their marriage was mostly uneventful, with the wonderful exception of Baby Louise.

Right before Louise was born, Rachael had a dream—it must have been a dream, but one so real she would have sworn it was if she'd been prone to superstition. Upstairs in bed, her pregnancy keeping her awake in the early hours of the morning, right at the edge of a foggy dawn, she saw that the shade was drawn over the east window. But the window filled with a golden light, and someone said, "May I come in?"

Rachael wasn't disturbed by this, it being a dream, and said yes. Although she knew she'd given it permission to visit, she really didn't want to see what was there, but the visitor seemed to know that. During their meeting, she never actually saw the spirit of Bridget, her young mother-in-law who had run away and drowned after abandoning little Harold. Rachael didn't remember her saying anything in particular—it was more of a feeling, like a welcome to their child and a kind of message.

Rachael kept hidden the memory of Bridget's spirit, to be brought out in case of emergency. She knew she would need its strength sometimes, although it took her breath away that any woman would desert her own child.

She drew on the power of Bridget to combat the harping memory of her own mother, who would never have let Louise get off so easy by marrying Gavin. "Stand by your child," said the spirit, "care for my little Harold as his mind weakens and the blue stars in his sweet eyes fade to pale water." For Rachael needed the patience Harold's mother never had.

Bridget had spent her first prairie winter in grieved amazement. It was a dry year, brown and harsh and bitter cold. The frozen ground seemed unnatural to her, and the wind at night sang in a chorus round and round the house. Frost shot from the nostrils of cattle and horses; barn cats turned up wide-eyed in death and stiff as toys.

She woke with a sore throat every morning. Her face itched constantly in the dry air. Her white hands were rubbed raw from milking, her knuckles cracked and reddened, and her legs ached from the cold barn floor. The springtime was not much better—the more snow, the worse the muck. Her husband and his father forever sweated to free up wheels buried to the axle and slid from house to barn to corral.

She'd once thought nothing could be worse than Ireland, scratching away in stony ground, growing up elbow-to-shoulder with brothers and sisters in their cottage, destined to end up old at thirty-five like her own mother. But Canada had a beauty so huge and wild and out of reach that it was meaningless. The forest vanished as Bridget travelled farther west to meet her never-seen husband, and her legs gave out when she stepped from the wagon and saw where she was expected to live out her days. Eighteen years old.

The vastness put a fear in her. After Harold was born, she began to experience an unfamiliar terror, and she'd wake in the night with a pressing weight on her chest: the Hag, there to suck her breath away. She knew she must leave that place, or soon there'd be no breath in her at all. *If I could get home, I'll come back when I'm stronger.* But what a punishment for leaving. Her husband, with his dark face, thundering, "No woman will be taking my son from me!" would have killed her before he'd have given up Harold. She ran for her life, but the Hag pulled a trick and took it anyway, a mortal trade for freedom.

Bridget understood the bargain she'd made when, at last, she was back in her country and found the copper-coloured pony waiting there in the hollow of the dunes. Her throat tightened when she saw its gleaming hooves. Hidden behind the creature's velvety features was another, older face, and that one looked straight into her soul. She crossed herself. *Mother of God, forgive me. I never wanted to forsake my Harold.*

Sweet Harold. She'd pressed him so hard into her apron that he'd pummelled her with his four-year-old's fists, "Ma, don't," in his tiny voice, ripping her heart to shreds.

"Be good now, Harold."

"But I'm always good," he said, making her laugh. "I'm always good."

CELIA CLOSED her locker door and thought: *Celia Protheroe closes her locker door with a ruthlessness that belies her gentle face, and with a grace honed by years of dance class, she braces herself for the bitter wind and prepares to embark on yet another lonely walk home: surrounded by many laughing friends, yet so alone.*

"See you tonight, Celia," Stacey's voice intruded as she went out the door with lanky Ryan. This created a new edge to the drama, more satisfying in its potential for some interesting bitterness. She really didn't mind walking home by herself. School was a necessary evil, an awkward place where the jokes she made with her family didn't get the same laughs, and the quiet persona she'd developed earned her a reputation as a snob.

The mysterious Celia wends her way home, crunching snow underfoot, gazing at the cloudless blue sky above, and, lo, someone is calling her name. Shit, I don't believe it, it's Jason.

He caught up to her in an easy, loping run. Her attraction to him embarrassed her; he likely wanted to ask about an assignment. But he stood in front of her, smiling. His silver tooth—odd but very cool—seemed to charge the vapour from his breath. He wore no gloves, just a cracked leather jacket.

"So. The inimitable Celia Protheroe."

"So, yourself." *Brilliant comeback. God, I've never actually heard anybody say "inimitable."*

"Going to McKercher's tonight?"

"Yeah. Actually, I'm driving some people."

"Want to hang with me a bit when you get there?"

"Sure." Celia tried to seem put out as if he'd interrupted something important. She kept her voice dead-level and lowered her eyelids, forcing her mouth to be still. But Jason grinned at her lips, then suddenly looked at her as if bored. She didn't resent that but studied him to see how it was accomplished. She knew his invitation was serious.

"It's nothing heavy."

"Of course, it isn't."

"We'll just get together."

"Sure."

This was the closest Celia had ever been to Jason's face. He had fair lashes and the strangest eyes, the irises almost gold. She had known there was something unnerving about them, that they were light-coloured, maybe icy blue. But there they were in real life, and weird, they were amber, like an animal's. But his pretty lashes allayed the wildness, and he pulled off his tuque and grinned as he scratched his tawny hair. She became aware she'd been staring at him and quickly looked down, only to have to look away again from his thighs, thick and muscled under tight denim, his legs dancing in the cold.

She had no doubt she stood next to a man, one barely seventeen. Jason was one of those guys who matured early: started shaving at fifteen, not the fine first hairs, but a full, scratchy beard. Unbelievable, the closest thing to being actually asked out—*want to hang, nothing heavy. Good. Nobody expecting anything in particular. We'll talk about different kinds of things. His cartoons are a little crazy this boy can really think he sees himself looking in from the outside like I do doesn't totally fit in. It's perfect.*

His lips fascinated her as they talked. She'd never actually wanted to grab a guy before and kiss his mouth as badly as she wanted to kiss Jason right then. But it was like he read her mind, and he laughed.

"What are you laughing at?"

"Nothing."

She needed to get out of his company, compose herself, get

home, and figure out what she'd wear. And, hope beyond hope, maybe tonight they could get a bit physical.

The afternoon light caught the golden stubble on Jason's chin. Her mouth was watering, like he was candy or something. Ridiculous.

"I've got to go right now, Jason. See you tonight."

He said yes. She'd seen him hop the bus going downtown most days after school, so Celia knew he was there only for her. As she turned away, she could feel him watching. She concentrated on her midriff, relaxed her shoulders, and strode from the hip until she reached the end of the block. Celia glanced over her shoulder. Jason stood exactly where she'd left him. He didn't wave, so neither did she.

THAT EVENING, Dion lay on a blanket, a quilted island in the eye of a storm of words and legs and colours. He ignored, as always, a dozen rubber toys that followed him around as his entourage, along with an old fashioned curly-furred teddy, utterly invisible to him unless someone put on a puppet show, where it became another blur in his landscape.

At four months of age, he had achieved something that comes easily to most newborns. He could raise himself up a little, his head bobbing and bobbing until it clunked down on the blanket like a blossom collapsing under heavy rain.

His eyes intently tracked movements, fixing on each person who stopped to see him. Head up. Bonk down. Dion's sisters took to calling him the Bump again since he landed on his nose so often, though it didn't appear to bother him much. Tonight, Morgan kissed his cheek and rubbed the top of his head. She brought his little seat and put him in it and because he was tired, propped his head with towels. Dion looked directly at her and she laughed for them both, thrilled at the unaccustomed eye contact with her little brother. Her laugh gave him a start, but he didn't cry. A thick string of drool fell from an ever-full puddle on his lip, and he sat in utter stillness, now concentrating on the tower of plastic blocks Morgan was building for him. As he stared, he felt a new stirring. He didn't recognize it as joy. Salmon, mint, delft, sunflower—the blocks were singing to him.

The song fragmented into tumbling confusion. Morgan's knee caught the blocks as she got up too fast. Dion heard the imperious voice of Celia, whose long dark hair was a living thing he wished he could touch, but how should he make it come to him?

"Morgan, if you don't do the dishes, I'll have to shower way too late, and my hair won't be dry. Don't be such a bitch. What are you doing that's so urgent?"

"Celia."

"Sorry, Dad."

CELIA PICKED up everyone she promised rides to, driving her mother's beat-up red Volvo, the one her friends called the yuppie car, in spite of the bullet sprays of rust holes on its door panels and an embarrassing number of miles.

She hung back after they'd taken their coats upstairs. She hadn't seen Jason on the way through, but even better, didn't notice his girlfriend, either. She looked into the dressing table mirror, licked her finger, and ran it along each eyebrow. Thick, like Gavin's, but she didn't mind.

Heavy bass vibrated the banister under her hand as she started back down.

"They said you were up here. Lucky me, I don't need to search."

Jason grabbed her hand and pulled her back into the

upstairs hallway. They sat against the wall for a while, talking, although not in the way she'd imagined they would. He sat close, leg to leg, shoulder to shoulder, as if they were already familiar lovers. Celia was burning up. Jason whispered that he knew where there was an empty room, and she followed him. The little bedroom had bright sailboat curtains and a single bed with a ceramic clown bedside lamp, and Celia wondered what child it belonged to. Music beat relentlessly through the wall, without melody.

There was a loud knock at the door, and she froze.

"I'm in here," said Jason. Authoritative. There was a laugh from the person outside, a boy.

Who cares. She stood, waiting. "Let's leave the light on," he said and grinned.

Celia loved his feral eyes, full of mischief and sex. She wanted to kiss him so bad.

They kissed. It wasn't quite what she'd figured on. It was as if his face was as over-muscled as the rest of him—his tongue was unbelievably hard pushing into her mouth, thrusting back and forth. And then he was all over her lips and her teeth. *Celia, Celia,* she thought. *Okay, this is another way to really kiss —I mean Jason has had lots of girls, he should know.* And Celia thought maybe she didn't know. She'd never seen the need to make out with a guy just for experience.

Celia waited for the timid move to her breast. But as they stood, Jason pushed her against the wall, and his hardness pinched against her pubic bone. He slid a hand over her jeans and pressed up between her legs into her. Intrusive, unexpected.

"Don't, Jason, not like that."

She was relieved when he laughed. "Okay."

But his hand was there again, and it hurt. He put an arm

under her sweater to grab a breast. Just like that. Grabbed it like he was pitching a baseball. *What the hell is this?* He pulled on her bum to press her tight up to the bulge in his pants, almost masturbating, the whole time kissing her.

Celia realized her cheek was wet and was disgusted.

"Let's fuck, Celia. I want you so bad, fuck me, Celia."

She froze. Saw with unexpected clarity the face of Jason, boy of her dreams. "Fuck yourself, Jason."

"Why should I? You're here."

"What is this shit? Quit it."

"Come on, you'll like it. I'm really good. Ask Lara, she's a real bitch in bed. Anyhow, you have to, look what you've done to me, I'm in pain." He yanked her hand to his crotch and held it there.

"I guess you'll have to suffer, Jason. I'm not in the mood for this."

"Fucking little cunt." He pushed her away. "Fucking little dyke. I was doing you a favour."

Celia walked out. She tried, she tried so hard, to keep her face relaxed. She breathed with the abdomen, she centred herself, she told her shoulders to give. She found herself downstairs, struggling with the sleeves of her coat, and could hear her friends.

"How was it, Celia?"

"Did the earth move?"

"Going already?"

And her own voice, "I guess. Yeah, I'm kind of tired."

Celia unlocked the old Volvo, got in, and thanked God for beat-up and familiar old car seats.

A knock on the window. "Hey Celia, how do I get home if you leave?"

"Figure it out, Stacey. I'm not your mother." She drove off.

How could I be so stupid how could I be so fucking stupid he's a total prick he'll be complaining to his friends right now and his breath was sour and I kept thinking it was fine because it was Jason he kissed all wet he was obscene. I should have known by that idiotic conversation in the hallway about girls having some special voice from Venus. Staring at him all year. Fuck it, Celia, how could you?. One more ignorant date to add to the DOA collection. Definitely the worst ever for being manhandled. Right up there with the dance where Ron and I sat and watched everyone for two hours and every word we said just sat in the air like a balloon.

A horn sounded behind her. She said, "Fuck off," but her heart pounded sickeningly. She looked in the rear-view mirror, confused, then at the green light before she understood what was required. She shifted into gear and the Volvo fishtailed just enough to clear her head, eased into third, and checked a street sign. Her turnoff was four blocks back.

Christ, and going home. "Did you have a nice time, dear?" All that crap about how unusual he was and how lonely I got, I wish I could get a big eraser and rub it out I could just die. What an asshole. Thank God I didn't cry or anything. Cunt he called me and dyke how could anybody be such an obnoxious kisser? Why can't I find someone? Right. Like I found Jason.

CELIA WALKED into the light of her house, a chaos of dishes and junk and books and piano practice and twins upstairs arguing, and it was like the peaceable kingdom. She looked in the living room and saw her parents, the ones who didn't do anything and didn't have a life and who she'd never be like. She saw them sitting side by side on that awful old couch and the television droning on with nobody watching it. And keeping her parents company with his feet on the table, womanless Roland, with the face of a rogue pirate, shuffling cards.

They all looked up.

"Deal me in?" said Celia.

SIX

February

Celia is searching for a party dress. It's here somewhere; she saw it before, the perfect one. There are racks and racks of dresses, too big, scoop-necked, ungraceful. She knows she is grown up, but Gavin gives her a little multi-coloured roll of cheap candy for her birthday, and if she doesn't find the dress they'll never understand she's an adult.

She is dressed. She has to hurry and get to the tea. Her dress is peachy-pink, with little buttons of turquoise in the centre of shirred taffeta flowers. She spins around and around, the skirt flying in a little umbrella about her knees. Princess Anne waits impatiently with the butler at a round picnic table made up with a silver tea service and white cloth, and the other guests frown at their plates. Why is she wearing this ridiculous dress? It isn't right. What will Princess Anne think? She is served three jellybeans in a dainty paper cup on a silver tray.

Gavin lay curled and rigid, his back to Louise. He is going up the sidewalk toward his house. The sun slips behind a cloud. He knows what will happen next. The front porch has turned to glass again, and the dead knight is here. It turns to him, imprisoned in the glass, black metal face menacing. It calls out to him, hollow-voiced and sad, begging, like every other time, for him to unlock the door. If he does, Gavin will find himself in the suit of armour, locked in the glass room. "Help me," he whispers.

GALE HAS FALLEN asleep on the couch. She hears a megaphone announce that the Bear will roar three times today. The air is sultry and oppressive, and there is a scent of terror. The Bear roars. The Bear is kept hidden in the lower level of town along a twisted street in one of the low, thick-walled houses. Its bellow fills the air, and Gale knows he roars for her, that if he were free, he would come right for her. She is going to the Bear. She has to. She is with a woman and a child in a tunnel, and she thinks if the Bear is free, he will eat the child first because it is sweet, and then she might have a chance. She is at the door of the room. His presence is so strong she can hardly move. She can hear him breathe. She can't bring herself to look directly at him. She can see the outline of his side and maybe a foot. He is a grizzly, and he is free. They are going to chain him to four women so that he can't move because he is being pulled in four directions. She wakes up and his presence still suffocates her.

MORGAN IS TALKING to Jessica's Uncle Greg. He stands so tall in front of her that her face is at the level of his navel, and his shirt is up, and his navel is full of fuzz. She is hoping he'll give her some money like he always does so she can get some Coke and chips. She loves him so much—he is really nice. But she needs to say something to him. She picks up a bottle of taco sauce and throws it up into his face so his eyes hurt really bad.

"I'm sorry it hurts you, Greg, but you have to tell my mom what you did."

"I didn't do anything to you. I never even touched you."

"Tell my mom what you did to me, Greg, or when I'm big, I'm going to kill you with a knife for sure."

Morgan doesn't feel mad. She is telling Greg something. Sometimes, she talks to him and kisses him. This time, she tells him. She knows she talks to him lots of times at night,

like this. Patiently.

LOUISE DRIVES DOWN A LONG HIGHWAY. The pines on either side go on forever. Suddenly, an enormous stag bolts out of the woods and the car is gone and Louise starts to yell out a warning to Gavin but realizes she's drawn attention to herself. The stag lowers his head and charges. She grabs his antlers and wrestles him into a building where men are sitting around drinking coffee. She calls to them.

They all look but don't move. She pushes the deer back outside and bends its head, and it falls, screaming weird, rhythmic screams.

THE PHONE WAS RINGING. Louise answered it, twisting the top edge of her sheet to wipe off the sweat between her breasts, barely making out what her dad was saying. "I said, Gavin. Let me talk to him." She did.

"Say, Gavin, Bob called and wants the number, the serial number for the car."

"For the car?" mumbled Gavin.

"You know where it is. Maybe it's on the registration."

Harold cleared his throat loudly in Gavin's ear, making him wince.

"What's the number for?"

"Insurance. Bob needs the number. Rachael answered the phone, and she was just scared as a rabbit, didn't know what to do."

"What was she scared of?"

"Didn't know what the number was."

Gavin looked at the clock. It was 6:45.

"Go back to bed, Harold, and I'll call you when I've got it."

THEY MANAGED to sleep for another restless hour before getting up for Dion. It was almost eleven when the three of them arrived at the farm to settle Harold, who had phoned again twice—in great agitation—during breakfast.

"Whose glasses are those, Mother's or mine?"

"Those are my glasses, Dad," said Louise.

"No, they aren't, those are Mother's," said Harold, his voice rising.

"I think she has hers on."

"Don't try to tell me that." Harold pointed a shaky hand in Louise's direction. "I know what goddamned glasses those are, and they're mine or Mother's."

"Now, Harold, my glasses are right here and yours are by your chair, look, where you left them, and those on the counter are Louise's for reading."

"Oh, say now." Harold stood quietly for a moment, studying the glasses, then sat at the kitchen table. Rachael set a little plate in front of him, muffin and cheese.

When Louise was a girl, she and Rachael often took meals out to the field. This was the only driving Rachael would do, jaw set tight, grinding gears along country highways and grassy road allowances to get to Harold's outfit. And sometimes, they took muffins and cheese and coffee in the late evening, way past Louise's bedtime, when the sun hadn't completely set, and Harold was working far into the night.

Harold would put Louise up beside him on the tractor. She'd bounce away for a few rounds, her ears ringing from the roar, worshipping this monstrous apparatus that forced the earth to churn and roll. And it was her own dad making it happen. And one cold May night, she left her mom in the cab of the truck and she ran across the hummocky rows of new-planted field peas and hopped up next to Harold. It was getting darker by the minute, and it was hard work to see through the grainy air. Bluffs of trees around the field were blackening into silhouettes. The horizon to the northwest had one pink glow that rose into soft yellow that rose into blue into deeper blue, and the tiny pale crescent moon hovered with the evening star bright to its right, just like she'd drawn it there. A fingernail and a dot.

They bumped around to the north, the east, the south, into the west, where the picture sky turned to darker, mysterious blue. And around again, circling closer to the big pothole, the one full of water in the middle of the field. There was a movement, almost invisible in the dusk. The head of a great creature rose toward them, followed by a body that swayed from the edge of the pothole on prehistoric legs. It walked slowly off with a huge, even gait, looked over its shoulder once to check the tractor, then dissolved into the dark.

"Dad. Do you remember that moose?"

Harold chewed on his muffin for a minute like he hadn't heard. But Louise knew to wait.

"Sure. In the pea crop that got hailed out."

She kissed his cheek.

Harold had been up since he called Gavin and Louise that

morning. Rachael tried to convince him he'd been dreaming about the car insurance, and there was no worry, but Gavin was the only person he would listen to. At eleven o'clock, Harold still hadn't got around to putting on a shirt but sat hunched over the plastic tablecloth, his broad chest sunken, brown nipples at the end of soft, breast-like muscle. His arms had thinned away, so skin hung in coarse furrows like the hide of an elephant. Most mornings, Rachael got after him to dress properly, but the business of the registration number was more pressing. So there were Gavin and Louise, restless, and Dion quietly staring from his grandmother's shoulder, all waiting in the heat of the Timmons kitchen.

Harold turned toward Dion with his mouth full of muffin, made a chewy Donald Duck noise for him, and laughed at it himself. He got up from the table and walked unsteadily toward Rachael, reaching out both arms as in supplication, and placed his own hands over Dion's tiny ones. "Warm me up; there's a good lad."

"Heaven's sakes, Harold, leave the baby alone and get a shirt on, you're positively indecent."

He leaned toward Dion and said, "Don't ever let your woman nag you the way this one does, boy. She used to be a sweet little thing, wasn't so broad in the beam in those days neither, and she could charm the birds from the trees. Look how she caught me. All it took was a little salt on my tail."

"That is the silliest thing I ever heard. Anyhow, seems to me you used a bit of salt yourself."

"Are you getting naughty with me at your age, Rachael?" Harold punctuated his question with a little slap to her rear end. Dion blinked.

Naughty. Rachael, who dressed in the bedroom closet every day of her married life, who never learned a proper name for any of her intimate body parts, and who now blushed to hear her husband talk this way in front of the family. She didn't feel deprived for not having a passionate marriage; she'd always found plenty of comfort in Harold's warm back against her own.

And here was Louise, their blessing. Never had she or Harold laid a hand on her in anger, or threatened her with God's punishment. And she was still a good daughter, coming here to put Harold's mind at ease, even though she had her own work to do. Rachael didn't know where Louise got the strength for it and giving birth to all those girls like they were puppies. *Look at her*, she thought. *Maybe a bit shadowy around the eyes —the sign of the resurrected—but a pretty girl still.* Well, now, not that it was her place to say, but you'd think Gavin might have left her alone after five daughters. But then, there would be no Dion.

Rachael laid her cheek against the warmth of her grandson's head, and he gripped her cardigan tightly with curled hands as if he understood the tenuousness of it all.

Harold slowly looked up and opened his mouth like he was about to speak. He licked the tip of a finger and turned back to concentrate on the last couple of muffin crumbs, and when he finally got them nabbed and finished off, said, "I guess I'll be taking Mother in to the Chinaman's after lunch."

Rachael clucked and sighed and handed Dion to Gavin so she could get busy with the dishes and drown out Harold's rambling.

"Which Chinaman is that, Harold?" Gavin flopped Dion over his forearm and sat himself sideways at the table across from Harold.

"Mother's vacuum is on the fritz."

"You mean that old guy with the store on 19th? He still in business?" Gavin quickly pulled in a foot, which threatened to trip Rachael as she stomped over to get Harold's dishes.

"You're thinking of Mr. Chin, aren't you, Dad, Shelly's uncle," said Louise.

"That's the feller."

Rachael clucked again and poured water from a rubber glove that had fallen into the suds. "Heaven's sake, Harold, why don't you speak English? It's just the belt's gone on the vacuum cleaner, Louise. Maybe you can pick me one up at Sears."

"Chinaman's cheaper," Harold growled.

Harold had discovered Mr. Chin's store years ago. In his shopping days, he'd avoided department stores, preferring the offbeat—pawnshops, the save-a-buck stores—any little home-made business. He'd pick up dishes for Louise when she was first married: enamelled tin, blue Wedgwood, old Canadian National Railway china with faded gold trim.

"We'll stop by on our way home, Dad, but I haven't been there in ages—he might have retired," Louise said.

More likely died, she thought. *It's been over ten years.* And Shelly—she'd almost forgotten about her. She'd come from the only Chinese family in their area, used to take the bus to Louise's school for Home Economics class, and always tried to get into a cooking group with Louise so they could talk. They'd moved away, Shelly, her father, and stepmother—an English-woman Shelly had said she hated. And what kind of name was that for a Cantonese girl?

Louise felt a stab of guilt. The last time she'd really thought of Shelly was when little Celia kicked up a fuss about how Louise dressed her, and Louise relented, remembering Shel-ley's parents keeping her in knee socks and tunics and under-shirts—how she'd looked twelve years old in her graduating class.

Dion fell asleep on the way to the city and snoozed along congested streets, past the pawnshops, the U-Save, the sex shops, the Many Mansions Street Mission Jesus Saves.

But as they drove by, Louise saw them all: people from the Middle East, from Indian reserves, Hutterite women in dotted kerchiefs and layers of skirts and thick stockings to keep out the winter, Métis girls with skinny legs and sweet oriental faces, women with permed hair and jazzy sweatpants. She had an urge to ask everyone if they were okay.

Gavin circled the block, looking for a space. He finally pulled over a hump of snow and backed in to park. Louise sat.

"Well, are you going in or what?"

"Yeah, I guess so. Gavin, does everyone look weird to you today? I mean, everyone walking downtown."

"They usually do."

"Usually. So why am I noticing them now?"

"Don't worry about it."

The hotel up the street was already doing a brisk business in the middle of the afternoon, the sidewalk corner filling with men, mostly, who didn't seem to notice the cold.

Louise got out and stopped to peer in the window of the Scientific World of Clocks. It was closed for good, although metal grates covered the windows and door, and hand-painted signs still advertised income tax services and old coins bought. She tried to look past the grates into the empty shop, but all she could see was her crummy self in the glass—a blur of traffic behind a tired face, hair falling from a braid, her nose red in the glare of the reflection. She'd grabbed whatever she could find that morning—elastic-waisted jeans worn the first few months of her pregnancy, beat-up crepe-soled boots. She shivered and thinking she sensed Gavin's impatience, turned toward the truck. But he was leaning back against the seat, oblivious, eyes closed.

She wondered if she would be able to stand it if Gavin lost his mind to something; if he became like her father. Would her love for him transform? Would he be like Harold, metamorphosed into some kind of pet? But, of course, it might never happen. Maybe it would be Gavin who was stuck with her. Where she grew up, there were men who abandoned their sick wives, or sometimes, when the men became widowers, they married the housekeeper. How hard had those couples once worked at discovering one another? How full of hunger and promises and gratitude had they been before the mysterious corrosion removed them from themselves to become she-who-now-lies-in-bed or father-who-mustn't-be-left-alone?

Louise turned away from the glass but had to quickly side-step to avoid bumping into a man who'd wandered into her path. He muttered to himself and abruptly raised an arm toward the street as if in defiance, then skirted her, wobbling on down the sidewalk, hunching deeper into his thin jacket.

Now she walked fast, barely glancing at the barbershop, toward the spot where Mr. Chin's used to be. Amazingly, Yes We Are Open swung on the inside of the door as she pulled on it, hearing the ring of a mechanical bell. And Mr. Chin glanced up from behind the counter. "Hi," she said. "I'm looking for a belt to fit an upright Eureka."

He stared at her for a second, then smiled. "Haven't brought your dad in here in a long time. Is he dead?"

Louise attributed this bluntness to a lack of facility with the language. "He's fine, thanks. Just slowing down a bit."

"Old age get us all."

"I didn't think you'd remember me."

"Sure I do. Shelly's friend."

Louise was almost afraid to ask. "How's she doing?"

"Great. She a doctor now and she marry a doctor. Live in Quebec and speak French."

"He's French?"

"No. Chinese."

Louise grinned and instantly wished Chanel suits and a big house on Shelly. "I'll tell my dad you asked for him."

She climbed back in beside Gavin.

"What are you looking so pleased about?"

"I think I've been in hell for a while. I think I just came out, and today was the last of it."

They drove across the bridge on their way home. "Hell is funny like that," said Gavin. "You don't always know you were there until after you've left."

Myrtle Murray is in a dream living room. Dion sits as an adult would, on the soft armchair across the room, gazing at her.

"Tell me, Myrtle, about how it was when you gave up your little boy," says Dion.

Myrtle remembers the ether. And the black oblivion of the birth, and shivering for days afterward, and the nightmares. And wide cotton binders tightly pinned around her chest to hold down the agony of engorged breasts.

"I didn't give him up, he died."

"No, he didn't. You know that because you signed some papers."

"I dreamed he had died, and they gave me another child wrapped in his skin to care for, a child who was orphaned."

"Well, that was me," said Dion.

"I'm sorry, I didn't know. It was a long time ago, and I was very young."

"I'm very young. Forever young. That's what it says on babies' tombstones. Forever young."

Myrtle woke up. Why did she feel so happy?

That afternoon, Twyla Jarosz sat on the fat hydrangeas of a reupholstered Queen Anne chair, a cup of Myrtle Murray's homemade rose hip tea in hand, visiting with her next door neighbour.

Myrtle hummed along with the sweet, meditative voice of Blossom Dearie, singing "I'll Take Manhattan." She stood tiptoe on a stool, reaching up to examine the purple vines of a Wandering Jew. She gently crumbled the paper of dead leaves into her palm and was reminded of the ashes of her husband, Edmund. Scant remains—she didn't know why she kept them. She had intended to empty the urn onto the dirt of the cutting garden so there would be bits of Edmund in every bloom, and she would have some earthly evidence of him.

Now, approaching her seventy-third birthday, Myrtle considered the possibility she might die at any time. Or be around for another twenty years, but she didn't know if she could wait that long before having a word with her Maker. She wanted it face-to-face. All right, God, what was the point? What was the sense in making me a mother? Why give me a taste of a man's love, then leave a child, not properly as love's gift but as my punishment?

Twyla had once informed Myrtle that she herself talked with the Lord every day. Sometimes frequently. These conversations gave Twyla the remarkable ability to be wise in all that she did and to always know what action to take, and should she err, the confidence that the Lord would cover her tracks.

"So the Protheroes are Catholics, are they?" she asked Myrtle.

"Louise was raised that way, but I guess you'd say she's lapsed."

"Good for Louise. You know my view of the Pope."

"Really, Twyla. I don't see the virtue in turning one's back on the perfectly respectable faith one was raised in. And who are we to judge whether all that confession and so on is good or bad for the soul?"

"She might as well be Catholic; they obviously don't practice any birth control. I mean, look at them. I don't know. I've heard the mouths on those girls, and I don't think they receive real guidance in any way, shape, or form."

Myrtle had a most alarming urge to hit her guest. "Well, Twyla, I'm sure you'll feel differently about things when your two are a bit older. And speaking of kids, how's your brother's wife coming along?"

"She had the baby a couple of weeks ago—she was over a

month overdue, you know. That little boy came home from the hospital eating pablum and meat."

"Don't tell me. Well, you'd think they wouldn't have let her go so long."

"These doctors, I don't know. My mother told me her neighbour's girl was too small, and the doctor wouldn't take the poor thing's baby early, and there wasn't enough room so it was born with crushed hands, and its head looked like a lima bean, but that eventually straightened out. But it never was right. In the head, I mean."

Myrtle had read in the morning's paper that, according to a British magazine, "weirdness was declining." She doubted it.

LOUISE WALKS SLOWLY through the quiet of a deserted battlefield. She has been in this place before. She recognizes the light that comes from both sky and earth; everything has the same muted intensity, as if the world is shrouded, leaving only the bleak hues of dried blood and grasses parched under thin cloud. This time, she can see two enormous earthen graves surrounded by water. The graves of giants.

Now she is unable to move but waits.

There is a woman, not yet dead, who lies there. The woman rises up, towering over Louise, and approaches. Louise is sick with fear and cannot watch but feels the press of an arm against her own, and she shudders. The woman grips the back of Louise's hand with fingers hard as metal. Currents of pain flow up her arm, and she is paralyzed. The only way to escape this terror is to plunge into deeper sleep.

LOUISE STOOD naked in her bedroom, looking awkwardly over one shoulder at a great black bruise that had appeared on her right thigh. She hoped she'd bumped into something without noticing, and it wasn't that this thing had spontaneously burst on her skin. Old lady leg. Louise was not ready for all of this.

Lately, she found herself experiencing sudden periods of obsession, constantly wanting Gavin to touch her, walking around in a haze that bloomed almost painfully. Louise felt possessed in these moments, a creature about to die, consumed by an urge to mate before she was overtaken. She had to fill herself before it was too late, feed her life so she could summon strength to battle the Hag.

She often lost focus for part of the day, but it wasn't as before; she swam in that place where thinking didn't exist and sensed an excitement, hints of things that might come. Like a chrysalis, she developed a shell, a detachment that protected her soft, undecided centre.

If Gavin was bemused by this heat in his wife, he didn't comment. Gavin accepted most of what life offered him, watched things come his way with the patience of a man fishing the same trout stream day after day, letting the fish reach him or pass by, as they wished. He had always been a willing lover and treated her with his usual tenderness.

And there was something new and lovely about Dion. He no longer seemed like an odd hybrid child, a human seabird, but finally, like a baby boy. He had become more as the others were as newborns. Time was different with him.

Louise believed he was going to be all right—there were capabilities waiting for him to find. The true miracle was he now looked a long time into his mother's face and she could see his recognition and joy. His purple-blue eyes bored so intently into hers that it sometimes made her laugh, and when she did, he'd jerk in surprise and throw his arms up in the air.

The twins quit asking if Dion was better yet. They could see he was healthy enough and were delighted to show him off to their friends, which—it puzzled them—didn't include the Weirds too often. They did wonder if Gale had scared them off, or maybe Margo had done the evil mother thing and told the boys to stay away.

The day of Gale's October tirade against the Weirds, when she finally got the nerve to bring the Bump home, her mother had met her in the kitchen. Louise was too quiet. Too calm. "We ate already; you can wait for yours," she said, and made Gale stand around until Dion was changed and on his mother's lap with a bottle stuck in his face, and he'd gasped and pulled back a couple of times while Louise made the sweet noises babies understand before he settled. As Gale waited, she imagined Louise holding the phone away from her ear to cushion the blow of Margo Weir's voice and how Louise might have apologized or maybe defended her. But Louise said, "Gale. You cannot physically threaten other people's children, no matter how obnoxious they are."

Gale's protests had stopped dead when she saw the wild blackness behind the green of her mother's eyes, the set of her mouth and the lines stabbing between her brow. She withdrew the question she most wanted to ask. *Is he really retarded?*

She understood that all those years Louise had hollered at her daughters, "This is the limit," it hadn't been at all. Only now, when the nightmare had come to pass, and she couldn't stop something bad happening to one of her children, was her limit reached.

Gale began to do the dishes without being asked, picked up milk from the store with her own money, and yelled at the twins to clean up their messes. She figured if there was something wrong with Dion's brain, then his brain needed exercise. She organized her sisters to put on puppet shows, to bring him interesting things, to read to him.

And the night Dion struggled to push himself up with his arms, and made it, he'd raised his head and looked right at Louise. She screamed in elation, and Gale took credit.

Even if he was retarded, he was still the Bump. Their Bump. Born as strange little Dion. Dion brought out a lot of instincts in Gale—she would die for him or for their mother. Face Margo Weir again. What did she care? But in daylight, she used stealth, approaching the Protheroe house from the west so she would avoid the malevolence waiting to break out from behind next door's front window, where she felt Margo eyeing her from the shadows like a moray eel, jaws champing.

DION PERCHED on his mother's hip, flopping against the length of her arm. He enjoyed this ride, even with her one hand uncomfortably cupping his cheeks as the other poured his grandmother's coffee. The voices of Rachael and Louise played lovingly all around the room, and every time his mother moved, he was spun into a new panorama.

He heard another voice. Gale was there now—he could see her. Then she was gone. Then Gale came back and got bigger and bigger and when she was big enough he flew all warm to her and she hugged him and she smelled like walks outside and he was so happy. He stared at her Gale eyes and watched the freckles hop around her nose.

"Little Bump, why are you looking at me like that?" Gale held him out in front of her and danced him in the air. Dion's face was perfectly relaxed, a baby doll with the kitchen light reflected off his lower lip.

She gave him a kiss before handing him over to her grand-mother. "I'm going downstairs to work out."

Gale whistled to herself as she slid her hands along the banisters. She made it down in two steps. There was only one civilized room in the basement, carpeted in gaudy red plaid, where they listened to music or watched the old television with too much green in the picture. There were various awful old pieces of furniture and the weight bench. A pile of crumpled clothes lay on one end of the couch. She put on a tape and cranked up the volume.

A voice from the clothes wailed, "Turn it off, turn it off."

"Jesus Christ, you scared the shit out of me. Get out of here and go whine somewhere else."

Morgan stuck her head out from under one of Louise's old coats, where she'd been curled into a little ball, and looked wretchedly at Gale, who only glared more fiercely at her. "Please, Gale, please turn it off. I feel really sick."

"Then go up to bed."

"Gale, I think I did something really bad. But promise don't tell Mom."

She turned off the music and sat down hard beside her little sister. "Forget it, I won't promise anything. So what the hell did you do?"

"Don't tell her, Gale. Never."

"What's the matter with you, anyway? Just don't go doing stuff that's that bad."

"Promise you won't tell."

"Maybe."

"I kissed somebody."

Gale laughed. "So what? And what else do you want to confess?"

"It was a grownup."

"What are you talking about? Don't be stupid, what grownup?"

"Jess's Uncle Greg. It's my fault, he asked if he could, and I said yes. And he kissed me right on the lips, and this is gross, he put his fat tongue inside my mouth. And he held on to my chest." Morgan gingerly put a hand on each of her tiny breasts.

Rage swelled through Gale and left her so dizzy she could hardly see Morgan. "Don't you ever, ever go to Jess's house again, Morgan, you hear me? Never."

"But Jess is my best friend."

Where was I, where was I, walking the fucking dog or something, and that creep was with Morgan? Look at her, twelve years old and stupid as hell. She could have been in really big trouble. She was. I'm going to kill him. How big is he? She didn't say. Maybe he's got a knife. Stop it, Gale, you're so stupid. Pay attention.

"What about Jess, Morgan? What's he do to her?"

"Nothing!" Morgan was horrified. "Why would he? He's like her dad."

"Not like our dad."

"Jess would say if something happened—we learn about it in health class."

"I thought you always said Greg was such a great guy."

"He is. But it's like there's two Gregs, and I didn't think about the weird one when he was being the nice one."

"If I find out you ever go there again, I will tell Mom, and you can watch her have a total nervous fucking breakdown. And Dad will call the cops."

"Cops, what for?"

"For what Greg did."

"He didn't do anything."

"Morgan, stay away from that freak. He'll do something worse next time. Everybody knows about those guys. Think about it. What sort of grown man actually wants to hang around with thirteen-year-olds?"

"Jess is the coolest person I know. She's going to hate me."

"Then keep being her friend. Just don't go to her house. Don't even think it, Morgan. I will tell Mom, I swear it."

Morgan sat cross-legged on the corner of the couch, miserably watching Gale do her stretches and start on the weights. *Why did Greg have to wreck everything?* She remembered sitting in the Dairy Queen and Jess so quiet and angry; maybe she knew something that night about what was going to happen to Morgan.

Then she got it. Gale was right about Greg and Jess. And what was really awful was Carolanne must know, too.

That was how it would be.

When Gavin came home from work that evening, he seemed amused to find Morgan drinking a cup of coffee in the kitchen with her mother and grandmother, talking to them about an article she'd read in an ultralight aircraft magazine. It was about the dynamics of an unrecoverable spin.

In the telling, Morgan felt she now had the power. She would be a pilot. It had been scaring her to death, all this talk in magazines of speed and altitude and tailwinds, but she understood the only reason some guy wrote about this stuff was so everyone would know better. She had it scoped, even if Rachael tapped her foot and stared out the window through most of the conversation, and Louise looked worried. Someday, Morgan would cut the engine of her aircraft and go into a stall on purpose. She knew how to prevent an unrecoverable spin.

GAVIN AND ROLAND sat in the living room, supposedly to watch Sunday afternoon hockey, but for the past hour, the screen had flickered noiselessly in front of them. Gavin's eyes wandered to it, unseeing. *Bloody Roland, like a hound on the scent, there's no shutting him up, no stopping him.* He drank absently at his beer.

"Gav, at the very least, you've got to be curious."

"What's the point? It was a long time ago."

"Maybe no point. It doesn't matter. Never know, you could unearth yourself a father while you're at it."

"I wouldn't know where to start."

"Sure you do. Register your name or something. People find their birth parents all the time these days, and then everyone gets reunited on talk shows."

Gavin snorted. It was all a game for Roland. Even when they were fifteen and had already spent most of two years together, Roland was somehow not around the night Gavin and another kid drunkenly broke into the back door of a confectionary, where the cops found them ten minutes later, drinking root beer and stuffing the fronts of their shirts with chocolate bars. Gavin was sent to Gillihan House for a while, where he played pool and did correspondence classes and ended up with another foster family. Roland always managed to be kind of wild without getting in deep; he'd never needed rescue or believed, as Gavin had at nineteen, he'd already endured too much.

"Even if I find her, there's a good chance she wouldn't want to see me. The whole thing might be a waste of time. What sort of woman would have her kid taken away or let someone do that?"

"Happens more than you'd know. I went out with Fiona all that time—remember? The social worker? She had real horror stories, and some sad ones, about kids they'd apprehended. From some pretty nice homes, too. Face it, the motherhood thing is over-done. The feminists tried to suppress any talk of maternal violence so they could forward their Men Are the Enemy cause. Mothers do some terrible things. But this woman probably had her reasons."

"My luck, she'll be the feature of the week on *America's Most Wanted*."

"Whatever. I still think it's good for a person to know where they come from. Of course, the flip side to that is you end up with too many peculiar relatives that you'd sooner not share the blood and bone with."

"Sometimes, I think I remember her wearing yellow." Or gold, maybe, radiant as a fairy godmother. But not in his dreams, which usually were sweating and grey, freakish things. "What does your book say about this black knight business? It happened again last night, a kind of three-act complicated one."

"If you really want to get into this, I suggest you find the whisky. And I don't have a book. Dreams aren't always a big deal, but I know if something really terrifies you, take it as a warning. That knight of yours sounds like a fucking spook."

Louise came in with an empty beer carton, which she filled as she talked. "Anyone happen to notice the language out here? Maybe wonder where my daughters get such ladylike mouths?"

She got dozy smiles in answer.

"This looks interesting. What have I missed, the transmission on the van and who's got parts at what cost?"

"You're good at this," said Roland, "but we did that already. We've moved on to motherhood and dreams."

"So esoteric at this time of day. Must be the hockey."

"Get us some scotch, woman, we're busy." Somehow, to Gavin, it seemed his wife turned around once. She wore an apron now and set two glasses and the single malt in front of them.

"Okay," said Roland, "what exactly is this thing?"

"It isn't a person." Gavin saw it. He always could. Metal, echoingly empty, trimmed with locks and shackles. "It's more like a haunted suit of armour, a being without mercy. And it waits for me in the glass porch." Not a ghost. He stared at the creature. He could almost hear it whisper back to him. "It's made of nothing but need."

Roland was quiet for a moment, pushed the hair off his face and said, "I wouldn't get excited; this spook is not so tough. You hold it in there with glass."

Gavin understood glass. Even drunk, he knew its properties. "Roland, you should do this for a living, you lost your calling."

"I hate school."

"I remember."

Sometime later, they simultaneously became aware of incredible food smells. "What's Louise got on for dinner? I'm dying here."

Gavin said, almost out of habit, "Get your own wife. Lasagna."

Louise frowned at the pair of them approaching the Sunday dinner in what they obviously considered to be a sedate manner. Fay and Hazel giggled, completely lost control, and ended up together under the table. Celia tried to look disgusted as she served the salad.

Gale and Morgan were the least disturbed. They'd seen worse.

The person most amused by the sudden gusts of emotion was Dion. He sat in "the crow's nest," a bucket seat lashed to the top of a high chair, where he could lie back comfortably and watch everybody. His sisters would say to him, "Ahoy Dion!", "Land ho!" and other seagoing sorts of things, and from that vantage, his eyes shone the blues of the Mediterranean onto his family.

"Louise, just then, when you glared us down with such devotion, you reminded me of my own dear mother," said Roland.

"I remind everybody of their mother. And drop the phony accent, Roland. Your mother's the most Ukrainian woman I ever met. And your father is about tenth-generation North American Irish, so that's no excuse, either."

"Third generation. You're so pragmatic, I don't know how you produced such a swarm of rare and gorgeous beings. Especially the little sprite here—reminds me of my Uncle Metro. 'Course, he was a terrible drunk, but no matter." He beamed at Dion.

Dion's eyes widened at the sudden vision—Roland's face of bold lines and high cheekbones flushed from humour and beer, looking at him with such delight it made him feel he was going to bust right open. Dion felt an unfamiliar quickening of the muscles in his face around his mouth. There was a spasm.

Roland's face exploded, rearranged.

"Good Lord, did you see that? He smiled. Right at me, I swear to God he did."

Before their dinner was done, Louise had phoned her parents and Myrtle Murray with the news. She marked the event on the kitchen calendar: *Dion smiled. Five months of age.*

They soon realized it was going to be tough coaxing him to repeat the act, but they all worked on it.

"I think the trick is you have to be talking right to him, you know, so there's nothing else to distract him," said Gale.

"You have to be funny, like Roland was," said Hazel.

"If Roland was any more of that kind of funny, he'd have a serious medical problem," said Celia.

"Curtis and Colin told me, and Hazel, their mom, said it was just gas," said Fay.

"Don't be stupid. Roland's practically an alcoholic," said Celia.

"No, I meant she meant Dion's smile."

"What a bitch, she has to try to wreck everything," said Gale. "I don't know how anybody could ever have wanted to live with her, even *Mein Fuhrer* over there."

SEVEN

March

Louise stood scowling out the dining room window into the dark.

"I hate it, Gavin. I go to the cosmetic counter, and they give me free samples of anti-aging cream. And did you see her at that store I've been going to forever, that towering new clerk with all the fat jewellery hanging off her?"

She swung around, blazed toward Gavin as if he were the culprit, and bit her teeth together as she spoke. "You know what she told me when I was trying on those little boots? She stood over me and said, 'A lot of women your age look really good in these boots; they're very fashionable without being extreme.' I mean, was I wearing a sign that said, 'This woman who has really bad taste is almost forty and has been off the planet for a decade'? No. I was wearing one of Celia's big sweaters and perfectly ordinary jeans. I hate it." She turned back to the window.

"Don't worry about it; you always look good. And in case you didn't look close enough at the women working in that place, they were all so made up you could see ridges left by the airbrush and putty knife. They chisel everything off at night. And I love the way you feel. You still have beautiful skin." He nestled behind Louise, rocking her as he warmed his hands on her breasts.

"I'm not ready for middle age. Maybe I should get my hair cut."

"Don't you dare. Your hair is a lovely black mist for me to lose myself in."

They watched the fine-grained snow blowing in great translucent sheets that suddenly swept upward into waves breaking, and they faintly heard, through the glass, the rattle of icy spray. "I've been thinking a lot lately about Myrtle. I feel so selfish; I've hardly spent any time with her. I really can't tell how difficult it's been for her without Edmund. You know how she always seemed complete on her own, so independent of him, with all her friends and that wonderful yard. But there was a balance in their house with Edmund around. I know she didn't have a terrible time letting go when he died, like that awful Twyla's mother did with Twyla's father. Myrtle was so, I don't know, normal about what happened to Edmund. And when she was given his blue jacket..."

Gavin had heard this part a couple of times before. There was something about it that fascinated Louise, although he couldn't see it, but he let her talk and rocked her gently.

"The one he wore in the accident. She washed all the blood from it herself. I've seen her wear it to the garden like she's wrapped in him."

"She's a very strong old gal."

Louise squirmed enough to loosen his grip and glared at him. "Why say 'old gal?' She's probably always been strong. It isn't like she gained strength through some desiccation process of the elderly, like an old piece of beef jerky."

"Where do you find these words, Louise?"

"I used to be smart. And you know what really got me is Myrtle saying that when she saw Edmund in the morgue, he looked kind of surprised. Like that was the last thing he experienced in this world. Surprise."

"Not too many people wouldn't be."

"That's what scares me. I don't want to be surprised."

"Quit thinking about it. It's not healthy."

"If we both died, who would there be to take care of everyone?"

They looked at each other, then laughed as they said, " Roland."

"Plus, Celia and Gale could handle things pretty well on their own," said Louise, "but it would be like some Edwardian novel around here, the Six Little Protheroes and their Terrible Struggles, useful moral lessons included."

"It's starting to blow pretty good—listen to that wind. Likely the last big storm of the year."

"It's barely March, Gavin. There's the whole month to go, and anything can happen."

Dion lay awake on his back in a willow bassinet next to them. He was the only one of their babies who had been able to use it at that age; the others had rolled around too much, snagging their knit baby clothes on the wicker, tipping it by peering over the edge or while trying to crawl out. But Louise kept putting them in there as newborns, she loved the look of it so much. It had belonged to Rachael, who slept there herself as an infant, and eventually was given to the little Louise, who tucked her yellow-haired Gretel doll into it at night.

Dion, being a bit of a doll himself, fitted the bassinet well. Many late evenings, he lay thus enclosed until his last meal before bedtime. He'd be taken from room to room, sometimes with piano notes falling all around or carried alongside a river of voices. Always, something was singing to him. At times, his sisters would appear, growing gradually larger, and interesting things happened as he heard them, so lovely with their happy and sad voices, so familiar.

That night, the howl and rattle from outside the house reached his ears, soft as a heartbeat. The rumble of his parents' voices warmed him.

"Look at him. It's like we get it better every time," said Gavin.

Louise stiffened. She adored Dion too, but here was Gavin, once again acting like nothing was wrong with this baby, and they'd produced some sort of privileged child. How could he be so stupid as to think Louise was unscarred, undamaged by it all?

"We get it better, Gavin? I think it was me bleeding to death in that abattoir of a hospital. I don't see that as an improvement on my birthing technique."

"It isn't what I meant, and you know it. Stop feeling sorry for yourself."

"Fine. You put him to bed. I'm not here."

Gavin could hear her angrily kicking girls out of the television room, and he knew it must be bad. She would stay there until long after he left for bed—maybe even spend the night on the couch.

He looked out into the dark and watched the snow cover up the windshields of cars parked along the street and blanket the walks until the silence of the house was disturbed by the beginning hiccups of Dion's crying. He quickly scooped him out of the willow. He was late giving him a bottle and dry clothes. Poor little guy, so patient and very wet.

Gavin couldn't even begin to count the number of diapers he'd changed in seventeen years. Louise had never pressured him to help the way he did, starting with Celia, but it was as if he needed to know what it was like. *If I was the mother, if I wanted to keep this baby safe and fed and always happy, how would I do it? Like this.* Roland used to get a kick out of his big friend fretting over those infants. Mother Gavin, he called him. When Celia was an indignant three-year-old, she yelled at Roland, "It's not Mother Gavin, it's Mother Louise."

The hardest thing for Gavin was that sometimes he could not stop a baby from crying. It distressed him terribly with Celia but less with the others. "Dogs bark, babies cry," his mother-in-law advised him. In fact, Rachael, who'd once seemed so dour to him, had become sympathetic, never critical. She seemed to understand his need to redefine the act of parenthood.

Harold, on the other hand, was highly amused by his son-in-law up to his elbows in the diaper pail or mowing the lawn with a baby strapped to his front. "Who's wearin' the pants in that house, boy?"

Gavin had done everything he could to make things right for his family, but injury had reached Dion anyway. It was bad luck or karma—they had no control over it, and there was nothing either of them could have done to save him from the damage. And Louise. He wouldn't even think about that. He told himself that an ambulance came for her right away, that she was in hospital within . . . how many minutes? Well, maybe longer than he'd admit, but she wasn't really in any danger. "We almost lost them both." That doctor was being dramatic, showing off, probably a medical student with a disaster-movie fantasy.

He returned to the window of the darkened dining room, where his face and arms assumed the camouflage of street light filtered by falling snow. The wind had died down, and he stood with Dion cradled in his arms, watching until his son's breathing became deep and whispery.

He went quietly up the stairs to put Dion in his crib. His own bed was empty.

Fatigue came in dark waves, but this was one of the nights Gavin was reluctant to sleep, uneasy about what awaited him. The birth of Dion had awakened a terror, one he had kept locked so deep he had thought it finally died.

Sometimes, before sleeping, he talked to his dreams. He told them what was too much—which image to keep from him, the voices to take away. But tonight, he was at a loss, powerless.

The alarm clock would go off in less than five hours. Gavin forced himself into bed. His back was cold where Louise should be; the pillow felt fat and suffocating. Dion was squeaking in his sleep, threatening to wake.

Gavin slept like a dead man.

"We're cold, we're dying. Me and Hazel want some hot chocolate. Where's Mom? My feet are wet. Hey, Morgan, the Weirds got a trampoline, and Colin and Curtis and us went on it all afternoon, and Mrs. Weir never bitched once."

"You should dress better. It's March, not May; there's still snow, for Pete's sake."

Fay stuck out a soggy foot. "We've got our woollies on, but they're not workin'."

Morgan smiled at her little sisters. She'd turned thirteen that week and basked in the spirit of tolerance that came with this new maturity.

"Fay, your socks stink," said Hazel.

"Oh, right, Hazel. Like yours don't. Plus, you've got a big juicy booger hanging out your nose."

"I was saving it for the collection on the wall by your bed."

"You two are disgusting," said Morgan. "And you'll have to

look after yourselves and get your own hot chocolate—Mom and Gramma went back to the hospital to see Grandpa."

Celia put her head around the kitchen door and looked into the porch. "You're all going to have to do something with this mess. I've got dinner to make and Dion to look after, and I don't know when anybody will be back."

"What about my socks, Celia? They're all muddy and stuck to my feet," said Fay.

"I'm not touching them. Just peel them off. Morgan, come watch Dion."

Louise steered Rachael through doors, up the elevator, and down corridors to Harold's new room, where he'd been moved from Intensive Care a week earlier. She often accompanied Rachael these days. Since Harold's collapse, her mother could not keep her bearings and became confused and upset by the simplest navigations.

Harold dozed with his mouth open, eyes half-shut, and an oxygen tube in his nose. Rachael went to his bedside, reluctant to wake him. Yesterday, he'd yanked out the tube and growled at her, "I don't need this damned pacemaker."

Louise nodded to the man in the next bed, his head a bottle-brush of stiff white hair. "A bit colder out there today, Mr. McAlister," she called to him.

"What'd ya say?"

"Did you have a nice sleep?"

"How's that?"

She ignored his beckoning motion. Even from that distance, the smell from his bandaged legs almost made her sick.

Harold had become restless, lifting a trembling arm and batting at his intravenous needle. Louise shook him gently and said, "Time to wake up, Dad, it's Louise and Mother."

Harold started and looked wildly around the room, but when he saw Rachael, his face softened. His eyes cleared. "It's you. It's you," he said and started to cry. He tried to give Rachael a little poke in the arm. If he could have danced, he would have.

He gazed at her for a time, consumed with an adoration that to Louise seemed pitiable and wonderful. His wife delivered her account of domestic news, all the time trying unsuccessfully to remove Harold's painful grip from her elbow. She gave up.

"Well, Harold dear, I suppose this means you won't be running off with one of those good-looking nurses too soon," she said.

"I think he's attached to you, Mother."

"Well said," exclaimed Harold, releasing his wife. "That's an excellent quotation." He smiled to the air for a moment, then muttered something.

"What, Dad?"

"Try the south road beside the lane. Try there, Louise."

"What do you mean?"

"I dropped it there. You go have a look."

Louise felt very lonely.

As in a dream, where the object of her search appeared only fleetingly and in unreachable places, her father—along with whatever he'd left on the south road—was mostly lost.

Till death us do part. Sometimes. Louise remembered the afternoon, years earlier, when she'd found her mother whimpering. "He promised to look after me, Louise, three times he made vows. Once at the church, and once only to me, and another after you were on the way. And he's leaving me anyhow."

"But he's right out back in the shop," Louise had said, though she knew why Rachael cried. She couldn't stand seeing her mother so weak, and at sixteen years of age was not willing to abandon her own childhood or to be abandoned. Maybe, more than twenty years later, she still wasn't ready.

Louise gave her father a kiss. "All ready to go, Mother?"

She turned around. Other than Mr. McAlister, the room was empty.

This was so maddening—her mother's impatience, the constant fretting and rushing. Louise had taken her to the supermarket the other day, and Rachael had had the door opened and one foot on the ground before the car completely stopped. It seemed to Louise that Rachael was trying to be one step ahead, so swift that nothing got a chance to leave her behind or catch her by surprise.

Louise hurried into the hallway, muttering, "Mother, for heaven's sake." She needed to overtake Rachael before she grabbed the wrong corner and vanished out of sight because who knew? In this place, it might be weeks before they met up again.

There she was, a little dark-coated silvery-haired woman scurrying off in the direction opposite to the elevator, fumbling with buttons and trying to close up her purse.

Louise caught up. "You might have waited."

"I knew you were in a hurry to get back to the children."

"I never said any such thing. And the elevator is down the other hallway. You'd have ended up who knows where."

It was hard to believe that only five months ago, she had caught Rachael in that rare moment of tremendous strength, where love transformed her as she cradled tiny Dion, and she was splendid—a saviour returned to comfort daughter and grandchild.

These days, Rachael dithered about like any helpless old lady, wary and uneasy, a bird who'd blundered through a window and couldn't find the way out. Was this it? Louise wondered. Would the sum of her own life's efforts be illness and a sense of dissonance with the world?

If she had asked Rachael, she would have known the measure of her mother's blessings. Firstly, surviving her own parents. And after that, having a man who bestowed on her his enduring love, who gave her one daughter, one son-in-law, and six grandchildren. Rachael's prayers had been fully answered. Almost. There was only a tiny one left.

She now prayed that Harold would go first—that he would not be left in this world without her to care for him.

EIGHT

April

It was two in the afternoon of April 9. Rachael swung wide the front door of the farmhouse, leaning into it as she surveyed her yard. Over eighty years ago, under that same porch, Harold's young mother Bridget had stood, stung by winds of a late April snowstorm; and before that, when the door was new, Harold's grandmother had folded her arms, as Rachael did now, realizing the week's rain had marooned her in a sea of muck.

Rachael looked out the doorway that afternoon not upon any adversity but only sweet air warmed by a true spring sun.

She walked out over frozen ground to the middle of the yard, where she remained for a time with her face tilted like a sunflower's, eyes closed, and soft old skin soaking up the gentle heat.

I am Rachael, and while I am able, this is mine to cherish.

Rachael found herself increasingly uninterested in events about her—the small crises of her grandchildren, Louise's complaints—as if she had somehow entered an unfamiliar country. She thought there might be words for what was happening to her, but she didn't know them.

Right now, she wanted assurance, to touch those things that had blessed her life since marrying Harold.

Her kitchen. As she might have cared for a longtime lover, she went all over it that day, cleaning and sorting, polishing her mother's old silverplate. To know it again. *I am here. Rachael Timmons. I erased my father's name and took the name of Harold's family, and this is my home.*

Year after year, she had planted a garden, fed chicks and then killed them to feed friends and family, and tried in vain to improve the south flower bed, where nothing but hollyhocks ever flourished.

Her gaze rested on the spot where Harold got rid of the skunk two summers ago. She smiled at the thought of him, stubborn and irrational, refusing to let her near the animal.

He had put cyanide in an egg and set the egg under the chicken pen. Rachael found the skunk a few days later, dead as doornails with its teeth in a frozen snarl. She offered to put it in the incinerator, but Harold became cross and said, "No, it'll stink for a month."

He'd got the wheelbarrow and the pitchfork, told her to go away, and threw aside the spade she'd given him; balanced the pitchfork on the wheelbarrow, hobbled off to get the skunk. Took him forever. Finally, got the thing speared and loaded, its wet scarlet guts hanging out and wobbling as he bumped along. The incinerator was filled to the top. Harold never wanted to set it alight; he was always worried about fire. But that was where he put the skunk, cramming it on top of all the other garbage.

And Rachael thought of her cat, Please Sir, whose death had not been registered in memory. She added this to her small list of regrets: that she had given in to her own upbringing and never allowed a cat in the house. There had been lots of barn cats, mostly stunted and sorry-looking things, and the few pretty ones a bit wild. Not like her tortoiseshell.

Maybe it was just as well. *Sweet cat.*

Fifty careful steps to the garden, including three she left in a north patch of snow by the chicken house. In the garden, alongside rhubarb and strawberries, twenty vertical ridges, twenty-four empty inches between each ridge. Every fall, she gathered and burned all the plant matter except self-seeding flowers on the eastern edge.

Two rows for onion sets, two for beans, three for peas. Peas by the bushel: pods opened, and tiny marbles rolled by the hundreds into a pail.

She thought of starting some asters this year, the giants.

And marigolds for a border. Never nasturtiums: the flea beetles swarmed all over them, turning them into rattling lace.

Her legs were cold. She headed back to the house.

Eighteen years earlier, Rachael had bought light rose paint from the Co-op in town and, by herself, trimmed the window frames and shutters and the crooked posts supporting the little porch roof. She looked now proudly, then regretfully, for the paint had baked in the sun and worn in the rain, peeled away in spots to bare wood, and the wood itself was grey underneath, and the grey was splintered and dry, and even if she had the energy to hold a paintbrush, wood like that couldn't tolerate paint.

My house has turned to old toothpicks.

There were sun dogs.

The moon was barely over the half, rising in the east, white in the spring blue.

· · ·

IT WAS seven in the evening of April 9. The moon was straight south now, almost on a level with the west sun, and was brightening—it would flood the sky that night. The sun dogs glowed behind a haze of indistinct clouds, ice crystals forming curved prisms. Wind from the east poured cold over the garden, cutting.

On the road by the farm, Rachael walked north. The sky lay in fractured mirages on the thin ice covering potholes and sloughs. She stumbled a little on the uneven clay road, rutted and hard, and so moved over to the gravelled edge. There, on the frozen surface of ditch water, she could see the overhead approach of Canada geese.

Rachael had been hearing them the past few weeks. The Stevenson boy down the road complained of his dogs howling as flocks flew over at night in the midst of March snowstorms.

The geese came. She stood, listening. One bird calling alone, *oo wonk oo wonk*. Then the beating of eighty wings, soft and percussive, so close to the ground she could see the curved downbeat—almost feel the wind they made, *whuff, whuff*, as they flew overhead. She watched three break rank and the flock arc toward the east, then straighten once more into formation, always north and north.

Rachael felt so good she longed to walk the mile and a half up to the Stevensons'. She might just make it, but if nobody was there to drive her back, she'd never manage alone.

Anyhow, Harold would be coming home in a few days. She'd better get some baking done—not that he cared much anymore what he ate.

When Louise had been old enough to leave alone for an evening, Harold and Rachael decided to get out and learn some proper dancing: a blissful evening once a week for five years with the Boom Town Ramblers Square Dance Club, Leah Stevenson's uncle doing the calling. Harold wore black trousers and string ties, and Rachael wore a gingham skirt with crinoline. In their last season, Harold began to have trouble keeping his feet straight and started to get the calls mixed up in his head. Rachael finally said, "Father's a little under the weather," and they never went back, except for the year-end barbecue.

It still bothered her she'd given up square dancing. Rachael had a passion for everything to do with it—the dressing-up, the ritual of movements, swinging to jaunty music, the caller's folksy humour. She might have found herself a woman partner, as some single and widowed ladies had done, but Rachael would not humiliate Harold. So, she went back to spending most nights at home, year after year, busy enough, the good Lord knew, with teenaged Louise and keeping house.

Rachael had been so absorbed in her thoughts she didn't realize the day had vanished, and she'd gone over half a mile down the road into twilight. The wind had died, but the dusk brought a chill that entered her bones and left them aching.

She was out of breath. The trees around the farm yard seemed far away and awfully black. Her chest was tight. She needed some tea.

Such a quiet road this was now, not like times when there were lots of families in the area, little farms on almost every quarter. A person could have real neighbours and parties with everyone invited, children and reclusive souls and bachelors included. One old fellow used to call on the Timmons right before Thanksgiving every year, bringing chokecherry wine, and Rachael would say, "Why, how thoughtful, Mr. Moore, and you must be sure to come for supper next Sunday."

Harold always said Mr. Moore was sweet on her.

When he died, there was barely a cent to be found on Mr. Moore's premises, nor did he seem to have a bank account anywhere. He'd already signed the land over to grandnephews. People came in the dark, looking for his secret stash. His little shack was stripped down to its frame, the floor torn up, and the yard littered with craters and mounds.

Rachael plodded toward home, wheezing, her ears ringing from the wind, legs numb, arms tingling as if she'd fallen asleep on them. She felt queasy. The moon was as bright as she'd expected from that afternoon, already drowning out little Venus in the not-yet-night. She couldn't remember if the outside light was on. She would get home, she would get inside, she would put on the kettle, and she would have tea and an apple muffin.

She wondered if old Alex Moore really had been sweet on her, but the thought of two men loving her was almost too good to believe and so silly she laughed at it. If Alex Moore had professed his love, would he have confided to her where the money was hidden? If there was any money, that is. Or would he have wooed her with his homemade wine, then turned mean and stingy after they married, doublechecking her household accounts and squeezing out pennies like they were gold pieces, begrudging anything spent on groceries and new underclothes? What a thought. She felt fortunate with Harold. And proud of herself for jilting Alex Moore, even if in theory.

Rachael quickened her pace, ignoring the fire in her chest and the weight of tired limbs. And there was the wall of firs— dark against grey—and the moonlit drive, and she was home.

NINE

May

____

Gale crashed into the kitchen, slamming the porch door behind her. She threw her backpack into a corner, sat down hard, and glared at Louise. "Never again. Never again. That is the last time I babysit for anybody anywhere for any amount of money."

"Settle down. I get the message."

"Mom, you should have heard those little shits. I mean, if you think _we_ have a problem with our mouths, those kids are straight out of a phony rap movie; they think they grew up in some Hollywood ghetto. 'Suck my dick, motherfucker.'"

"Gale!"

"That's exactly what they said, I swear it. And the boys chase their little sister around all macho, 'Get the bitch.' And the bunch of them look like they never ate a vitamin in their lives. There's moss on their teeth. I gave them popsicles, and their teeth turned orange. They are demon children. Ugly demon children with purple around their eyes." She scrubbed at her sweaty bangs, making the centre stick straight up. Louise decided Gale looked exactly like she had when she was four: cowlicked short hair and hot-faced mad.

"Did you at least make some money?"

"Oh, yeah, I got paid, you better believe it. You know what's in their living room? Bottles of coloured water. I swear it. That's how they decorate their house: old wine bottles filled with water and food colouring. I nearly went insane—there was nothing to read except the Sears flyer.

"And they've got this huge television the guy won some-place, with like a ninety-inch screen on it. And a couch that's worse than our basement one. And plastic chairs. They both go to work—what in hell do they spend their money on? She comes home today, 'Oh, thanks, Gale, are you busy next Friday?' You bet I'm busy—for the next millennium. But I said some dumb thing about exams. I can't believe those are Twyla Jarosz's friends. I cannot believe she'd hang around with anyone like that—she's so religious and everything."

Louise wiped a pile of counter crumbs into her hand. "I think they go to the same church."

"I've seen some lame excuses for kids before, but nothing like those three. And the oldest one, that's ten or something, came at me with a letter opener. Don't laugh—it was a metal thing with a blade. I said, 'Did you want me to feed that to you, Blair, or what?' He says, 'Ha ha, lesbians are real tough girls, hey Gale?' So I say, 'I'm not a lesbian, and even if I was, it's not your goddamned business.' Then, can you believe, he says, 'I'm telling my mom you swore, and she won't pay you, and anyhow, Charise don't like you, do you, Charise?' And Charise sticks her face at me and says, 'No, I don't like you,' like her brother's some big hero. There is nothing in that house. What do they all do? Hardly any food in the fridge, and weird cereal and boxes of junk in the cupboards."

Louise set a heated-up plate of spaghetti on the table. Gale pulled her legs in and sat sideways, rolled the noodles around her fork and griped as she dug in.

"And that woman gives me twenty bucks before she leaves and says, 'Oh, Gale, would you mind taking this to that yellow house across the street? Ryan accidentally broke their basement window last week.' Her snot-nosed seven-year-old walks around like Rambo with a homemade slingshot—I myself had to take away his BB gun—and he breaks someone's window a whole week before, and his mother waits for me to pay up for her? Then she tells me how she gave him such a licking. Shit, she weighs about three hundred pounds—I'm surprised she didn't kill him."

"Are you done?"

"I don't think this is funny. Hey. Why do you look so nice?"

"Fay and Hazel's band concert at school."

"Move over, Benny Goodman, it's the swinging Protheroe twins on clarinet."

"Since when do you know anything about Benny Goodman?"

"Late movie. Do we all have to go?"

"It would be nice."

Gavin had to bribe his daughters with the use of the Volvo and extended curfews before they'd promise to watch the twins' band. Friday nights, even for Morgan now, were sacred. He understood. Free, though it rarely happened, for him to stay up late, maybe drink too much.

He'd driven Hazel and Fay an hour ago after rounding up clarinets, regulation white turtlenecks he hoped would fit them next year, and black pants he knew wouldn't. He tried to hurry the others. Rachael had spent the night and was making a final call to Harold as Myrtle washed the Protheroe dishes. Like his daughters, he'd rather start Friday night differently.

They found a spot in the front row and sat shoulder to shoulder, "Auditorium" stencilled on the back, to be kept alert during the concert.

Dion was strapped to his chest. Eight months old and heavy. When the twins were babies, they wouldn't have put up with this; they had squirmed and yelled through dance recitals and Christmas pageants and kindergarten graduations. But the Bump had been fed and should be content in his marsupial bag to stare or sleep.

The auditorium filled. Gavin spotted Celia, Gale, and Morgan, haughty and womanly, near the back. They didn't look his way. He searched the stage until he found Hazel and Fay perched on the edge of chairs, waving madly at him. They were beautiful. Pointy-faced and toothy, big runners on the end of skinny legs.

Gavin tried hard to visualize himself when he was nine but couldn't. He wasn't able to remember where he lived or recall whether he might have been interested in music. Who would have come to watch? As he did, obscenely proud and satisfied.

Hazel's eyes were darkening, and she chewed on her lip. "Relax," he wanted to tell her, "nobody sees but the ones who love you." Too late—she had the giggles.

Dion jumped against his heart. Gavin looked down. His son's eyes widened at Margo Weir's piercing voice.

"How's your dad, Louise?"

"He's back at home and much better, thanks."

"What?"

Dion started again. Gavin kissed the top of his head and thumped his back softly. The Bump's eyes fell upwards. His lips made a round moon and then closed.

Gavin glanced back at Margo, brilliantly lipsticked beside

her husband, then turned to the children on the floor in front of the band—too old to sit on laps, a frenetic, jostling, nose-picking mass. Beside them, a lone little boy of about three rolled in oblivion, back and forth, a log caught in mysterious rapids.

He felt Louise, next to him, swing around in her chair. "He's at the farm now. He's pretty weak but doing fine."

"Your mother is a saint, Louise. If Larry ever gets that bad, he's going to a Home, aren't you, dear?"

"Not the same one you're in, I hope, dear."

Gavin laughed and stopped himself, but Dion slept, radiant and deadweight, unimpressed.

He muttered, "Hey, I could almost learn to like that guy." It was said for Louise's sake; it never bothered him, as it did her, to dislike a person.

The band teacher tapped his music stand, fiddled with his tie, and tapped again. The log boy wailed as his mother scooped him from the floor, and the band blasted, not entirely on cue, into a song from *The Jungle Book*. The nosepickers said *oooh*. Finally, the twins stood with four other clarinetists for a solo. Hazel missed some notes, biting her mouthpiece, trying not to laugh, but managed to choke out two lines from "March of the Tin Soldiers." Gavin heard Gale's whistle from the back of the room, thumb and forefinger between her lips. Must have got that from her mother's side—he couldn't do it.

LATE IN THE MORNING, Harold emerged from the downstairs bathroom. He walked gingerly, head thrust forward, lungs whistling faintly, fingertips finding a wall or cupboard door for balance. The Fruit of the Loom label stuck out in front at his waist. "Heaven's sakes, Harold, what are you thinking? Get back in there and put on your robe."

He stood and stared at Rachael a moment, each breath

carrying a bit of soft music from his chest, then cleared his throat, pointed at her, and said, "Hardy-har-har" before going back the way he came.

Rachael saw the cotton fly of his underwear bulging irrelevantly over his skinny butt, and remembered how modest he'd been when Louise was growing up, the extremes he took that his daughter never saw him without clothes. She sighed as she heaved herself up from the kitchen table, clucked her tongue, and sighed again on her way to help Harold get right-side-in and frontwards.

"We'll be outside," Louise said to the closed door.

Back in the garden, Louise and Gale found Gavin already finished with Harold's traditional job of marking rows, parallel and straight as pins. Louise grabbed a packet of carrot seed from the box and said, "See if we can do it before they get out here." Another garden ritual dictated that Louise use her talent in planting all tiny seeds, a job that always frustrated Rachael. She poured a little mound into her cupped palm, mixed in garden dirt, and half-ran down the row, letting the mix sift gradually into the fresh scraped row.

Fay was the human measuring stick, lying between each of the small hills Hazel shaped and planted with six vine seeds. Pumpkin done. Zucchini done. Spaghetti squash done. Fay was extremely cheerful about it, painting dark streaks under her nose and making angels in the black dirt, plugging up her nails and rubbing grit into the scalp lines between her braids.

Gale and her dad fiddled with chicken wire on splintered frames, setting up fences for sweet peas and runner beans. Rachael arrived, cradling a bowl of soaked bean seeds. She said to Gavin as if he'd recently met the family, "I just don't remember getting the garden in so late. You know, Harold and I always plant by the third weekend in May."

Gavin nodded agreeably. Gale rolled her eyes and hissed at

him, "If Gramma says that one more time, I'm going to scream. Anyhow, why do I always have to be here for this? I hate it. Every year, it's the same thing."

"Settle down. It's not every year, and it isn't like your grandparents can't use your help," Gavin said.

They could hear Rachael ordering Louise to put a barricade of string around the ornamental corn to stop Harold, who, over the years, had carefully tried to weed out Rachael's flowers and any unusual vegetable.

Tangent was dragging a rag around the yard, his tail up, head up, very proud of himself. There was a shriek from Hazel. "Bad dog, drop that right now." He ran toward Louise with the thing hanging from his mouth, a pair of men's underwear, and as she tried to grab it, he ran backward, tail wagging.

"Drop it," ordered Louise. He did, and she picked it up carefully and took it to the burning barrel. She wouldn't bother Rachael with this one. Harold arrived in slow motion and started giving orders, but the garden was done. And it was beautiful, clean and black and ordered—beets chard peas green beans radish lettuce onion carrot parsnip corn potatoes.

Rachael called from the back door—the stew was ready on the stove. As he walked to the house, Gavin was planning his grace for the meal, it being Sunday and required.

He had it. *Lord love us.* A quote from Myrtle Murray, who used it breathlessly in response to a good joke.

TEN

June

Hazel balanced with one foot on the kitchen counter, one propped against the sink. She gripped the edge of a cupboard, her head bent sideways, squinting up at something through the window, and shrieked, "Mom, hurry up, there's bird babies under the roof, three of them. Mom, hurry up, they're puppet babies." The stretching necks were tiny arms that operated the bobbing, turning heads, an absurd fuzzy wig on top of each, and three tiny hands held wide the yellow-trimmed mouths.

Hazel squealed again, "Lookit, the mother's got a worm. Hey you! Hey you! feed the other guys." One head vanished into the nest, leaving two blindly searching upward.

"Don't worry about it, she'll get more."

"No, she won't. Hey, stop her! She's sitting right on top of them. She'll squish the really little one. I'm going up there to poke her off."

"You leave them right alone. That bird knows what she's doing, and nobody's squishing anybody. But get outside anyway; it's too nice to be in here."

"What if the Weirs' cat eats them?"

"Nothing but a monkey could reach that nest."

"I'm a monkey. All right, all right, I'm going."

"Gavin, are you dressed? We've barely got an hour."

Louise put on her makeup in the car. The funeral wasn't due to start for almost another two hours, but she didn't count on her father being ready, and Rachael's scurrying and fussing usually slowed things down and got Harold more flustered.

They found him in the kitchen, struggling with the jacket to his good grey suit. "Well, here's the calvary and someone looking very pretty."

Louise kissed him. "Thanks, Dad."

"Look here what your mother got me." New brown suspenders were clipped to the trousers. "Does the trick, and they feel pretty good too."

Rachael called down the stairs, "Father thought faith was going to keep his pants on for him."

"But Faith left me for another fella. That's the way the cookie bounces, eh, Gavin."

"Maybe you should quit getting these religious girlfriends, Harold."

"Now, there's a thought. Mother, your face on yet? We got the chauffeurs here champin' at the bit."

Louise noticed that even Harold's good trousers had a little dried spot of food or something on the side of one leg. Rachael wasn't as careful as she used to be; they would find traces of meals left on the dishes, crusty half circles under the rim of mugs, things put away unwashed in cupboards.

Rachael came downstairs. "Life goes on, but it's never quite the same, is it? You know, Leah Stevenson and I used to pick chokecherries and saskatoons together . . . well, that was a number of years ago now, but the thought of it. I've lost so many neighbours. Seems like our only outings these days are to funerals. It makes me feel funny. Leah and Fred were married in June, and Fred went not ten years later in June, and here it is Leah having her funeral in June."

Louise reached over and smoothed a heavy patch of rouge on her mother's cheek.

Rachael tilted her head. "All right now?"

"Fine," said Louise. "I just thought of something. How was it I never had a Trousseau Tea?"

"Well, really, Louise, where did that come from?"

"I guess Leah and Fred. And I remembered my Wedding Party cutout dolls and colouring book. You know."

"I think, if you'll recall, Louise, you weren't even sure the ceremony was necessary. I could hardly sleep for nights on end. And if you had told me you'd wanted a Tea, I'm sure we could have arranged it. But you had a perfectly lovely wedding."

"Yes, I did, and all the right people were there. Anybody who felt like coming, plus all their kids, and an elegant buffet catered by your church ladies."

"I thought it was lovely food."

"It was."

"Really." Rachael folded several tissues into her purse and snapped it shut. "I just don't know if you're serious sometimes."

After church, they drove in procession out of town and past the underused Catholic cemetery. Louise listened to her mother's commentary on the service: it was lovely. As was the

eulogy given by Leah's granddaughter. As was the music, although Louise saw Rachael poke Gavin, who snorted when the nervous soloist hit an off note.

Louise once told Gavin to throw a big dance when she died, but he said he likely wouldn't be up to it. Every funeral she'd attended bothered her. She tried to envision the perfect one. There had to be ritual and mention of the guest of honour, but the only thing she could decide was everyone should be buried under a new tree.

They followed country roads to the Protestant cemetery and parked in rows against the fence. Louise thought, *Now this is a fine place to be buried.* No sounds but the drone of the highway a few miles off and a bellow from a corral. And the wind.

It was no longer the days of the hat, so the south wind parted the mourners' hair at the back as it wrapped skirts and trousers snugly around them: chess pieces placed about the grave.

A young woman sang "Amazing Grace" as Thomas Stevenson and his wife and son and daughter each placed a rose on his mother's casket. Louise was only thankful at that moment that it wasn't yet Harold or Rachael lying there, for that singer at the graveside might be Twyla Jarosz with her best choir voice on, and Myrtle might come laden with gladioli to give the Protheroe family, who would place them, stem by stem, on the polished wood.

She noticed lines that sprayed from the corners of Thomas's eyes, cross-hatched on his cheeks. *He's dying, too. Everyone is dying.* Louise felt something grip at her chest but knew it was only the remnant of the Hag, a poor echo of the flapping image of death that had no business here, in this place that required stillness and affection. And as the grip relaxed, she was surprised at the weakness of the fear's hold—it had become a shadow of itself.

Louise looked at her bent little dad, curling like a dry leaf on a vine, and was reassured.

She wondered if, when the time came, Myrtle's precognition would stand by her, if she would be forewarned. But what would it matter? It would serve no purpose. Or had it helped Myrtle? Did she treat Edmund differently in those few days between her dreams and his accident?

The wind softened. Late sun grazed the tops of the flowering shrubs at the edge of the cemetery, all at once illuminating hundreds of floating seeds that spun in a lazy vortex. Louise nudged her mother and pointed.

Hazel had gone outside as she was told but not before grabbing Fay to come with her.

They were powerfully in love. Hazel suspected it wouldn't always be so, but for now, their loyalty was uncompromised. They delighted in camouflage, one mistaken for the other by almost anyone outside the family.

Louise often showed them photographs of when they were little. In many of these, they held hands and usually were dressed the same. But Hazel, for some reason, had always worn blue, while Fay got an outfit in contrasting green or red. Hazel knew this was going on but kept it a secret until the last birthday—after the friend party with hotdogs and treat bags— the family one, where they opened packages from their grandparents. Hazel was so polite. "Forget-me-nots," said Gramma, on a cotton nightie with blue slippers to match. And Fay got an ivy print and pale green slippers. "Trade?" said Fay. Then Hazel knew she knew and traded.

They stood in French braids and cut-off jeans, craning their necks, standing between their house and the good-neighbour fence on the Weirs' side. It was difficult to see the round nest under the eave by the kitchen window, and the mother robin divebombed them a few times before they finally caught a glimpse of babies. They were entranced by the cheeping from the nest and wondered why they had never heard anything like it in their lives.

"Maybe she had her nest someplace else. Like the big tree by the back door or something. I don't get it. How do they figure out how to fly? Or do they know how when they're not babies anymore?"

"Yeah. That's what they do. They grow up and fly someplace else."

"Do you think the mother cares? Like, does she come home one time, and there's no birds there?"

"I don't know. She looks kind of stupid."

"I think she wonders where they went."

"Maybe they don't go anyplace. Like, when you see a whole flock of birds, the babies are there, too."

"Yeah, that's right. They fly around, and then they go south."

"That's in winter."

"Yeah, that's right. So they play all summer and eat worms."

They watched until something tiny bit Fay's ankle. She scratched and said, "Got any money?"

"Why? Want to go to the store?"

"Something else. Should I dye my hair?"

Hazel squealed, scandalized. "What colour would we dye it?"

"No. Just me."

Hazel quit laughing. "If you get to, I get to."

"I mean so people could tell us apart. So they'd say, 'Oh yes, Fay is the one with the purple hair.'"

Hazel wanted to cry. "Like Celia did, and Gramma had a fit? But then you'd have purple hair, and I wouldn't get anything. 'Hazel is the one with the boring hair.' And anyhow, we don't even look the same."

"Everybody thinks we do. 'Which one are you?' It makes me mad all the time."

"Me, too. But I get to dye it a different colour, okay?"

"Okay. So, how much money do you have? I've got a dollar and my penny jar."

"I bought the slushes, remember."

"What's dye cost?"

"How should I know? Ask Celia."

"She'll get bitchy."

"Her friend used Kool-Aid—that Darcy when she looked like the princess doll—she said she used Kool-Aid."

"We've got some."

They looked at each other and said, "Okay."

An hour later, Hazel and Fay stood on a pile of stained, wet towels in the bathroom.

"It's not very orange," Fay said.

"It's kind of. When the light hits it."

"It doesn't look like Darcy's."

"Maybe she left it on all night so it would soak in."

"My hair feels hard."

"What if we wrecked it? Fay, Mom's going to kill us if our hair stays hard."

"And kind of orange."

"Yeah? You really think it's orange?"

They peered into the mirror together for the hundredth time.

"Yeah, it's orange. But it feels pretty shitty."

"No kidding."

They heard a yell from Celia. "What in hell is spilled all over the place? Hazel and Fay? Come here right now. Shit, my feet are sticking. You guys have tracked all over the house. Mom's going to kill you. What's this crap on the counter? Hazel and Fay, answer me—I know you're home. Get into the kitchen this second."

They came downstairs, grinning, and stood in the doorway, sophisticated, nonchalant.

"What do you think?" asked Fay.

"About what."

"Our hair."

"Looks the same to me. Except dirty or something."

Hazel braved a reply. "We dyed it with Kool-Aid."

"That stuff in the cupboard?" Celia started to laugh. "It's ninety-nine percent sugar—you'd just make syrup. You guys better take a shower and then get out the pail. I'm not cleaning this up. God, I never wanted to dye my hair when I was your age. There's hope for you two yet. Listen. If Mom says it's okay, we'll get a rinse from the drugstore and do it right. But don't get all thrilled—I won't even ask unless you wash this floor. And the bathroom, too—I bet it's worse. Promise right now."

Something was happening with Dion while nobody was looking. It was the first June of life outside the womb, nine months old, and he lay in his crib, where everyone thought he was sleeping, but the brightness was too attractive for sleep— the flicker of leaves in sunlight, voices and voices downstairs, thumpity sounds on the stairs and voices, but no one came to see him. Hazel and Fay were outside yelling about birds, but the mosaic of noise didn't explain that to him.

He saw funny things in his mind's eye, things that made him happy. He would have reached them where the jumping-around voices were if he could. He wanted to move then. The flannelette blanket had been kicked off, and he worked his arms and back so that he felt a rocking, rocking, and somehow every-thing tipped, and he bumped his face on the bed. He didn't understand how it got there—he was all by himself. But he'd been on his face before and knew to push hard with his arms and work so he could see straight out; his head bobbed and bumped down and bobbed, and one arm collapsed, so he lay curled on the shoulder. It made him really mad. So he called for somebody. *Somebody, somebody change this now.*

Gale was there. "Bump, shh, stop screaming, shh. Didn't bad Celia put you on your back to sleep? You're all sweaty, poor little guy."

Dion soaked Gale's shoulder with his snot and drool, and he was happy, but it took time for his body to know that—his body still made mad noises. And he hiccupped for a while, all happy, while Gale showed him Out the Window, and Spin Around and Give Him a Hug. Gale had freckles, which he loved very dearly and were very chatty on her face. Gale fixed him up to make him cool and dry and took him thumpity down the stairs and gave him a drink from the bottle, the funny other taste and the sweet. Gale liked to sit and talk and talk. "Bump, look at the picture, see Miffy in the plane," but he could only see Gale's nose. So he touched it and that made her face smaller and she laughed, so he smiled, because he was good at that now, and everyone in the world smiled back at him.

If Gale could go to war for the Bump, she would. If Gale could wrestle an archangel, the one who pokes his nose into the affairs of mothers, she would. Because Louise talked

to her about *abruptio placenta*, and Gale envisioned a Latin or medieval condition that she believed had to be met on fantastic grounds, where time could be rolled on a spool backward, and she would win the battle, and she would say, "Now Louise will go into labour two weeks early, and this ripping out of my little brother's lifeline will not happen, you hear? Because it took so long for him to breathe that tiny parts of his brain died right there, and we can't get them back. I know. I've tried. I have really tried. And he is so sweet and smart and it's a dirty trick that other people don't know that."

When Gale dies, she wants to become an avenging angel and has made plans that if there is God, she will apply for that job, even if she has to miss out on Heaven. And she will swoop into the lives of people who hurt children and make them stop however she can, even if she has to blow out their brains.

ELEVEN

July

The wind blows cold on Gavin. He is standing apart from a crowd of people, strangers, who seem unconcerned with the surroundings or the danger. They stand on the grassy ridge of a mountain, encircled almost entirely by miles and miles of peaks and grey cloud. They talk and move closer together as they prepare for the climb up the last hill. It towers in front of them, almost vertical, fitted with wooden stairs. He is sickened at the thought of going with them but has somehow become a part of this tourist group.

They climb quickly and casually, so he goes along with them, horrified at the broken treads, and reaches the top, where he is too frightened to look, and then back down. He waits.

The others are gone but for one. She approaches him. He thinks he should know her, an odd little woman. She stands less than two feet tall, costumed as if for a garden party, in a tiny dress suit and wide boater hat that hides her face. Something disturbs him, but her size gives him courage, and he tries to shoo her away. She doesn't move but motions to the hill, forcing him to go up again.

Now, the stairs are even steeper, perilously narrow. He can see clusters of houses miles below as he climbs alone, and the wind pushes at him. The stairs have become less than a ladder, just bits of wood stuck into the awful slope. He climbs with urgency, feeling a menace at his back. Exhausted, clinging, he looks down to see if the little woman is trying to follow. And he sees her face. Huge and horrible, charging up the hill, closing in on him with crushing speed. He screams with no voice.

Then he hears Louise, and he finds a place where the thing could not reach him. And Louise holds him, compelling even his tears into silence.

At three in the morning, Louise had been awakened by a sound so soft she thought she'd imagined it. She listened a moment and heard it again. *Gavin.* She looked at his eyes, which stared, half-opened and blind in sleep. Then he seemed to struggle, his arms jerking rhythmically like a dog's limbs in a running dream. There was terror in his low moan. She said quietly, "It's okay, Gavin, it's all right, it's all right now, don't worry, *shh.*"

He squeezed his eyes tight and said, "Thank you, oh thank you," and Louise knew she'd rescued him that time. She said, "Turn around, and I'll hold you." So he did, like a little child, and she pressed the length of her body against him, wrapping round his back, her knees tucked behind his, one arm under his pillow and the other cradling him until the shuddering stopped and the breaths that were catching on the verge of tears quieted.

Gavin fell into dreamless sleep.

Louise held him until her right arm was numb and thought of how she'd lain with the Stevenson boy like this after they'd tried to make love.

Sixteen years old, walking out on the Half in search of Harold, who'd gone out with the tractor and crazy harrows that morning and was very late for supper. He would be found somewhere behind the west bluff a mile down the field. The Stevenson boy, fifteen, was with her. Black hair, violet eyes, same as Elizabeth Taylor's. "Fists like hams, that boy," her dad had said.

He still lived down the road from her parents' farm and was called the Stevenson boy even now, although, like Louise, he was almost forty. And he was a grandfather by virtue of his seventeen-year-old daughter. Rachael would start on the subject of wild little Cheryl Stevenson, "In my day . . ." but always stammered to a halt under Louise's glare.

Louise and the boy, Thomas Stevenson. His head ducked as he spoke to her; a laugh ended every sentence. He wasn't nervous but glad, as she was, to be tramping over this field this evening, only the two of them. His dog Toby came along, introduced as a one-quarter-coyote collie lab shepherd and who also, said Thomas, ate rat poison for breakfast, oatmeal laced with warfarin. And Louise's first pup was with them, a border collie, doomed to be backed over by the tractor. But not that day.

What did they talk about that evening? Louise wondered. What were the things they said to one another that, she remembered, made her want to run like the wind? She knew it was possible, running like the wind—she'd done it. And heard Harold say he'd done the same as a boy. Levitation, almost. "I flew once," Harold had said to her. "I know it sounds nuts, but I did."

Louise knew it wasn't nuts. You'd run so hard your feet didn't need to touch ground: they'd skim, a brush of sole to earth every eight or nine feet.

Toby was bullying the pup badly that evening, flipping it over and stepping on its belly, putting his jaws over the little muzzle. Louise finally carried it, leaving smears of black dirt all over her jean jacket. She and Thomas walked side by side toward the distant sound of the tractor and saw the haze of dust rising up behind the trees. They reached the corner of the bluff where water had lain a couple of weeks earlier, and Louise told him about some moose prints she had seen there, so big she could fit her foot in one of them, and she asked what would happen if Toby flushed a moose out of the trees. Thomas said he heard that they liked to attack heavy equipment, like the tractors clearing out deep bush for lumber companies, and they sometimes rammed buses on mountain highways. If one came after them that night, there would be no place to hide, nothing to duck behind or under on the prairie. Just old barley straw, furrows and hummocks from last year's crop, and the fence line a quarter-mile away.

How would it feel to be trampled to death? Great Ice Age feet. The wattle, brown and flapping velvet as the beast charged, eyes the size of golf balls. Antlers like carved tables. Would they gouge or spear or just flatten you? The legs. You could drive a small car under those legs. How could the prairie have such a monster? It didn't seem natural.

It was the only animal she ever worried about. Sometimes, she found a coyote watching her calmly, keeping a distance, not seeming to run if she or the pup moved in its direction. They used to be called prairie wolves, maybe taking a calf or lamb or kid.

If a black shadow moved oddly across the field, like both dog and deer under the illusion of distance, she would whisper, "Fox." The pup would light after it, chase it for miles, never getting near it. She saw red-haired kits one time, their den hidden under the thatch of brome grass by a road allowance, rolling over each other, grabbing tails and showing tiny sharp teeth, oblivious to Louise. Being ferocious.

She didn't see badgers too often, like little wolverines, solitary, elusive. Harold took them on a drive down a rambling summer road once and caught one in the headlights. Amazingly fast, running two-dimensionally in front of the truck, a flat creature on the shortest of legs. At least, she said to Thomas, there were no bears; she'd read they run like racehorses. Racehorses with big sharp teeth, he had said.

It's odd, Louise thought, *the fears one remembers.*

The Stevenson boy had a cousin who visited one summer.

He was sixteen when she was ten. Way too young. And he kissed her and said, "Promise you won't tell anybody, and I'll kiss you again." But she told Thomas Stevenson, who reported back to his cousin, and his cousin said sternly, "I'll never kiss you again, Louise," making her ashamed.

And Thomas's grandfather had told them about an Indian effigy he found years ago in his pasture, a piece of land long since sold to neighbours. Its image was still strong with her, and the word "effigy" overlayed itself upon other things.

She remembers thinking it was a scarecrow. But it was fieldstone, carried piece by piece from somewhere and placed in the ground. The grandfather, or someone else, had made a sketch of it, like a child's gangly drawing of a person. Nobody seemed to know much about it and thought it could be like a road sign marking that place for tribes on their way by. A sign saying what? Plowed under by now.

But Louise and Thomas had searched for it and had lain together in the cool shade of poplar and badger brush on the edge of the pasture, trying what lovers do. Beautiful Thomas, lying in humiliation. Louise held him for a long time, having her first sense of what being a woman might be like. "Don't worry, *shh,* don't worry, we'll try again."

Old Mr. Stevenson had plucked stone axes from the fields he tilled, using them as paperweights and doorstops and bookends until one weekend some visitors from Ontario admired them and took home all but one. He had made a collection of hundreds of flint arrowheads, all sizes and colours—some had been sharp enough to cut paper. All lent and lost.

And that evening, as Louise and Thomas eyed the trees nervously for charging moose and wandered toward the tractor's swelling roar, they somehow found themselves sunk past their ankles in soft mud. Stuck like burrs.

They laughed for ages as they struggled their bare feet out of ooze and fished for wet black socks and caked shoes.

That night, they sat side by side on the porch steps, each wrapped in an old blanket, chaperoned by Rachael's intermittent appearance at the kitchen window. Northern lights arched across half the sky, a double veil of soft green fringed with rose, the constellations misting behind. They stopped whispering now and then to hear the lights crackle and, later, the howling of coyotes.

Thomas Stevenson. Friend for a while, love for a week. *Here lies the Stevenson boy's love in memory.* It should be like that for everyone at least once in their lifetime.

She carefully pulled her arm from under Gavin's pillow and kissed the back of his neck.

TWELVE

August

"Louise, I need to clear out the cellar. Is there any possibility of giving me a hand this week? I don't know what to do with it all—so many things to decide in a job like that. Some of those preserves must be good still, but how can you tell? I can't see throwing the jars out, but there's a lot of them to unseal and scrub out. It's been nagging me. I don't want to leave a mess for somebody when I'm gone."

"Where are you going, Gramma?" said Hazel.

"Your mother knows what I mean. And now that you're all here, there's something else." Rachael rummaged through a few drawers. "I was certain . . . oh, here." She held up a roll of masking tape. "I want all you girls to tell me what you'd like to have when I'm gone. Now Louise, if something happens and I'm with my Maker before Harold, well, I don't think your father will be able to manage on his own. Of course, the nurse visits, but she can't be here three meals a day, so you'll need to find Harold a more convenient place to live."

"What's Gramma talking about?" asked Fay.

"Dying," said Hazel.

"She's not dying."

"No, like Mrs. Stevenson. In case she does."

"Hazel and Fay, stop whispering and come help me. I want you to take a look at the cups and saucers in the china cabinet and show me your favourites so I can put your names on them."

"Don't do that, Mother; you'll want to use those for company."

"Nobody likes a cup and saucer these days, Louise. A mug is easier."

Fay was making little hot *uh-uhs* with her breath as fast as she could on the glass door, seeing how many steamy spots were left before the first one faded. "Hey, can I take one home now?"

"No, dear, they belong in the cabinet."

"I don't want a cup."

"You'll appreciate it when you're older, Hazel. And I know Louise will want the Singer treadle." She wrote *louise* on the tape in red felt marker, tore off the strip, and stuck it under the sewing cabinet.

"Mother, please, we don't need to do this. Forget it; we'll worry if the time comes."

Celia was peering through the decorative wire grating on the doors of the old Chinese chest. "Can I have this?"

"Only if Louise doesn't want it. Do you, Louise? I remember when my mother picked that up at an auction sale—I never thought it went with anything."

"If Celia wants it, it's hers," said Louise, somewhat disgusted with her mercenary daughter.

Rachael sighed. "I suppose most of this is junk. I don't suppose anybody really needs any of it."

"Not at all. You have lovely things. I just don't want to see everybody's name plastered all over your house. But if it's okay, I would appreciate your books."

"Aha. See? Now, Gale, what would you like?"

"I'd like you not to die."

All of a sudden, Hazel brightened. "Hey, I know. Can I have your car?"

"That's it. Enough. We're going home right now. Hazel, run outside and find your dad and grandpa. We'll do this another time, Mother, I promise."

"Well, I'm going to make a list."

"Good idea."

THIRTEEN

September

Louise puzzled for a minute at the centrepiece on Myrtle's coffee table, a huge spray of last year's bachelor buttons and wild grasses set in an oddly familiar brass vase. "My God, Myrtle, is Edmund under all that foliage?"

"No, he's finally in the garden. Do you think it's too much having the urn in here?"

"It is a bit gruesome. I think it's the sort of thing people would recognize."

"I was afraid you'd say that. I didn't know what to do with it; it's not something one gets rid of easily. I thought, now, if Louise spots it right away, it will have to go. But if not, then I'll keep it full of bouquets. But it would be, I don't know, sacrilegious to store it or give it away. I never thought I would be so sentimental. I was so proud of myself this morning. I woke up and said, 'Edmund, it's time you were laid completely to rest. Go where you can do some good, and I will have you with me every day of the growing season.'"

"So exactly where is he?"

"I don't think I'll tell you, Louise; I don't want you getting squeamish whenever you help me in the garden."

"It might be wiser to tell me, otherwise all sorts of things become suspect, and I wouldn't want to do anything irreverent." Louise envisioned brushing specks of Edmund off her knees, rinsing him down the bathroom sink, or leaving streaks of Edmund under her nose when she scratched it in the garden.

"He is well dug in if that's what worries you."

"Hadn't even occurred to me. And I promise not to be squeamish, but as for the urn, I think you should keep special bouquets for yourself and put it back in your bedroom."

"I'll do that. Then, really, nothing will have changed—he'll be with me as always. Now, before we start getting morbid, come out back, and I'll show you the wild cucumber. It's the most beautiful seed—I find it quite fascinating."

After fifteen years of visiting Myrtle's garden, Louise knows she can still be surprised. The very first time she came by for a visit, Myrtle already had the coffee percolator plugged in and said, "I had a feeling you were on your way," and Louise thought, *Yeah, right. Batty as hell.* Myrtle then further irritated Louise by saying, "Now, tell me all about yourself." She'd felt like saying, "If you're so clairvoyant, you tell me," but gave her usual tense little routine about staying at home to look after Celia and infant Gale.

"Gale, ah. She is a stormy child."

"She's got colic."

"Exactly. But from the looks of her, she'll have it for life. Not the stomach ailment. It's her bursting inside that causes her pain. She has a very strong spirit, this one, and needs to grow into it. Watch out for her because she won't ask for help; she's the type who wants to do it alone."

Two-year-old Celia was sitting quietly on the floor that day, stacking and restacking measuring cups, stirring things with the wooden spoon, tunelessly singing bits of a made-up song about "Jack and the Beanstalk."

"There's your family's daydreamer, who believes everything is possible."

Louise was thankful Myrtle's moments of psychic inspiration were rare. She didn't think they could have been such good friends otherwise. Neither would she have taken those times too seriously. But coming as they did, erratically, sometimes uselessly, it never overwhelmed Myrtle's good character. She had never used it as a weapon, as people sometimes did with gifts, especially ones of faith or intelligence, and had never presumed to be right about everything because of her supposed privileged knowledge. She was an unusually observant woman with the sort of common sense Louise liked.

In the garden, Myrtle held her hand out flat so Louise could see what she thought was so beautiful.

"They look like some alien eggs, all brown and hairy and spiky, like something out of *Day of the Triffids*," Louise said. "I mean, it's a nice name, wild cucumber, but they're savage-looking things, aren't they? A bit sinister."

"Really, Louise, no wonder your mother worries about you."

"Rachael worries about everything—it keeps her going. I don't know about these; I was thinking more of a nice vine, a clematis or grape, even some of your Virginia creeper, then I wouldn't need to coddle it over the winter. I have a hard enough time keeping things healthy even if they can yell when they need something; although these look like they might be able to talk, maybe slink into the house at night and say nasty things to us in our sleep."

"The leaf is lovely; it's got a nice strong shape. This is a beautiful climber, sends out lots of furry little tendrils, and forms loads of seed pods so you can put it wherever you need some cover. It's really marvellous."

"See? What did I say? It wants you to aid its wicked plot."

"Fine. You're welcome to some Virginia creeper. Excuse me, I'll run in and grab the phone."

Myrtle came back to the garden, looking annoyed. "It's Twyla, having some little crisis with her lawnmower. You haven't been to her place, have you? It isn't much like yours; she's rather a fussy housekeeper."

"Thank you."

"You're quite ornery today, Louise. Tisk tisk. And be nice to poor Twyla."

The Jaroszes must have used lots of weed killer on their lawn to keep Myrtle's natural yard from contaminating it. Big hothouse geraniums sat on either side of the front step, the only relief to a gravel border running the length of the house. Twyla met them at the door. "Ignore the mess. I'm having one of those days where things keep getting away from me."

The front hall was decorated with a ceramic "Bless This House" and a "No Smoking" sign. Louise followed Myrtle's example and carried her shoes. She wasn't sure what mess Twyla meant unless it was the sewing machine and bits of fabric and thread scattered on the kitchen table.

"Sorry to rush. Next time, I'll serve you girls coffee, but Bob will be back at five-thirty." Their stockinged footsteps were deadened by the thick blue carpet.

"Robbie's room. Jamie's room."

"You must know something I don't, Twyla."

"Oh, heavens, the boys would leave things all over if I wasn't after them. Anyway. They were fighting, you know how it is, Louise, and of course, they kept bothering me when I was trying to finish the back lawn, and finally, I had to sort them out. Master bedroom."

Blue and more blue, a sharply made bed, frilly his-and-her lamp shades.

"And I hate to upset Bob. He works so hard."

"He works Saturday?"

"Well, no, it's his golf day, but I made him late this morning with the mower." She gave a tense smile. "And basement. Television room." Checkered sofa and chair and shelves with bowling trophies, laminate woodgrain tables.

Twyla tiptoed to another door and opened it enough so they could duck their heads in. "Bob's toys." Almost a whisper.

Louise would have loved to play there. It was a little room with clouds painted on the upper half, the lower in mossy brown, completely taken up with an elaborate HO-scale trainset and a world to go with it. But Twyla was already halfway up the stairs, saying she had to get back outside.

"So, what's going to upset him? Am I missing something?" asked Louise.

Twyla's voice was rising. "Like I said, he fixed the mower already, and I promised the grass would be done, and, of course, once you stop, it has to get jiggered with. The cord doesn't stay wound or something. I don't know."

"I'll give Gavin a call."

"No, don't. Bob would have a fit if he found out I bothered him."

"What about bothering us?" Louise wondered aloud.

"It's not the same." She went deep red. "I mean, I hoped the three of us girls could figure it out."

By the approach of five, Twyla was almost in tears. They had the top off, but no amount of jiggering would coax the cord to retract. Louise was pretty testy. After all, she'd come to mooch plants from Myrtle in exchange for helping clean the perennial bed. She waded through Twyla's protests and apologies and phoned Gavin.

It took him barely ten minutes, but it wasn't fast enough. They could hear the garage door open and close, then footsteps.

Bob stopped. He stood about five-eight and was on the pudgy side, his face round behind conservative glasses.

"Gavin Protheroe," said Gavin, extending a hand.

"Oh. I've heard Twyla mention you. We, uh . . ."

"Just came by and helped your mower."

"Thanks very much. Shouldn't have broken down in the first place, right, Twyla?"

"Hell, ours used to do the same damn thing. Got rid of it."

"DON'T LOOK SO WORRIED, Louise. She'll be fine," said Myrtle as they headed back to her garden. "I quit giving her advice ages ago. She'd call back every time, armed with reasons for disagreeing with me. You, on the other hand, will listen, which is how I know you are smart."

"At least I don't let some fat little man patrol my life. I'm astonished at my tender thoughts for Saint Twyla."

"You can't save everybody, Louise. I tell Twyla the same thing. Of course, you have entirely different missions in life."

"Hadn't thought I was on a mission."

"Don't get defensive, dear, but you spend a lot of energy trying to cushion people from the world." Myrtle reached into the netting tangled alongside her shed, and snapped a few pods from the wild cucumber. "Try a couple."

Louise held them gingerly. "It's worse than before. Look, they've got disgusting eye sockets."

"You know, I had the sweetest dream about you the other night. You were roller skating past my house, and I waved and thought: *There goes Louise. There goes my friend, Louise.*"

SHE WASN'T hard to find.

An uncommon name. But his mother had married, they told him. Where was he when that happened? Mrs. Gwendolyn Miller, nee Protheroe, now fifty-six years old. A child when she'd had him. Father Unknown.

He had been driving northwest, alone, for almost seven hours. Gavin. He held on to the word and tried to lay it over the dissolving faces of unknown men until he knew that he was named for his grandfather, dead a long time ago.

GAVIN SAW THEM. Once upon a time, the man and the little girl. The man sings to his daughter as they roll slowly across the Atlantic, and Gavin thought if he listened hard enough, he would remember those songs, but the words swirled in wind and spray, brushed him as they slipped by, and were lost at sea. While the man aches for his wife, he tells the girl stories to quiet and soothe.

And they land in Halifax. The man and little girl live. Where? They live in peeling boarding houses and on cold farms. The man speaks a coarse, lilting English. And soon, they live wherever the mines are and then the logging camps. The girl grows and learns the language she needs. And one day, when she is old enough, the man does not move aside but stands still and watches a tree that is about to kick his jaw so hard it breaks his neck. And the girl is given some money.

THE NEXT MORNING, Gavin met Ruby, the district nurse who would take him to his mother. He'd pictured Ruby as petite—her voice on the phone had been childish and breathy, and she laughed at nothing—but she was an abundant woman, multi-chinned and dimpled at the elbows.

She shook his hand and blinked furiously. "Oh, well, look at you. I'm sure I can see a family resemblance there. Listen to me. Of course, there would be."

He barely noticed the town. Gravelled streets and some new bungalows, but mostly modest little houses, almost cottages. They slowed by the Municipal Water Treatment Plant—a mound beside a boxy brick building. Next to that stood a thick hedge. Gavin waited under the shadow of lilacs at the yard's entrance. The sidewalk was cracked and heaved, the lawn patched with poverty grass and creeping Charlie. He could see it clearly now, the tiny grey house that had been almost invisible from the street—sided in asphalt shingles, encircled by elms.

Three faded wooden tulips were the garden. Ruby went to the door, which opened, and she spoke to someone for a few minutes before returning. "Go on. I'll be right here," she said.

He was at the door, knocking. Could see a dark shape moving within. Heard a voice. One he hoped to recognize but didn't. "Well, come in."

Even through the screen, he could smell something, and when he stepped inside his eyes stung from it, an ammoniac stench. He could hardly focus; everything seemed to have one colour, one texture. The first thing he saw was a kitchen witch swinging gently round and round above the sink. He didn't understand what made it go. And then he noticed a fly swatter in the woman's hand.

There was an indefinable movement everywhere as if the house was swarming, a current which gradually materialized into cats. Countless cats, surprisingly healthy, and Gavin realized he had heard them without knowing it, a white noise of purring and yowling and scratching. There were two wrapped around the woman's thin legs. Her bare feet were splayed and calloused; the nails needed clipping.

Gavin looked at her face. He was shocked to see it was almost lovely and again shocked at its familiarity. She had what Rachael would call good bones, a beautiful profile, with his same high-arched nose and full lips. Her housecoat was yellow, although not the yellow he remembered. Her hair was the colour of webs, and caught back from her face, and as she turned to swat the fly by the window, he saw she tied it back with a wire and paper fastener, the green kind from a garbage bag.

The glory of being in her presence almost overrode the powerful smell.

"The nurse told me you wanted to see me." He could hear, now, the barely perceptible inflection to her voice. Welsh. "Christ knows why. So. Now you've seen me." Her eyes narrowed. She stared up at him for a moment. "I'm not stupid. I know exactly who you are."

"I'm Gavin Protheroe."

"Protheroe, is it? Haven't heard that name in a long time."

The bathroom and bedroom doors gaped into the kitchen. A cat hunched on the toilet seat, drinking. A litter box spilled on the floor. Gavin looked back to his mother.

"I'd thought I'd seen the last of you," she said. "In fact, I hardly believed you'd ever been there at all. I thought maybe I'd made you up. I've been known to make things up, you know."

"They told me you've been sick."

"I've been sick lots. I've seen more in my short life than you'll ever want to know." A quilt fell off the bed in shredded tatters. More cats crawled out from under it. There were cats asleep on the kitchen counter. "You look like somebody I know."

"I'm Gavin."

"I'm not stupid." Her voice became shrill, louder. "Don't

you ever, ever, for one minute, think I'm stupid. I've got more brains in my little toe . . . nobody calls me stupid."

Her nostrils flared, and as she took a step toward him, Gavin remembered she wielded a fly swatter. He stood his ground and immediately felt foolish. This was a slight woman, almost sixty years old, barely up to his shoulder.

A tabby kitten mewed at her feet.

"Look at the pet. Look at the precious." She clicked her tongue, and the kitten purred as she picked it up. The fly swatter dropped to the floor. She cradled the kitten in both hands and rubbed it all around her face, her eyes closed.

Gavin's stomach clutched. He was falling, feet first, slowly.

"Hey. You look sick. Don't get sick in here. If you're sick, you should go away."

"Gwen Protheroe?"

"Not anymore, I'm not. I told you, I don't know that name anymore. That worker told me that name once, and I said, 'Listen, that's behind me. I don't like that name. I'm a Miller now. A married woman. I am a married woman.'"

"Where's Mr. Miller?"

"Who?"

"Your husband."

The kitten chewed at her hand and batted her fingers. "I've got to feed this thing before he eats me." She laughed, then abruptly, savagely, kicked the other cats out of the way.

"She said you'd like to see me."

"Who?"

"The nurse, Ruby. She said, 'Yes, you would like to see me.'"

"Well, now I've seen you." She opened the fridge door.

"Do you want to talk?"

"I don't like to talk."

"Then why'd you say you wanted to see me?"

"She said I had a boy. She said the boy was looking for me. I figured I knew what was up soon as she said that. As I explained to you already, I thought maybe I'd dreamed it."

She dipped a finger into a can of cat food and said softly, "Here it is, here. *cariad*."

Gavin felt pain behind his eyes. The kitten greedily licked her fingers.

She looked up, right at him, and laughed. "You thought you had a fairy godmother someplace, didn't you? Look at you, you're a grown man, you're practically bloody old as I am. What do you care about all that nonsense? Why in hell would you want a mother?"

Fairy godmother? Maybe. God, how could this woman have guessed so much? How he'd buried hope, hid it way behind his secret thoughts; hope barely formed as the unadmitted fantasy of reunion with the woman who had given birth to him, who would embrace his children, fold them into her wide skirts, make everything all right. A woman whose features were concealed.

"If I made a mistake once, well, that was mine alone to make. And when I was relieved of my burden, I said good riddance to bad rubbish. And if that isn't what I said, well, I should have. I could have any man I ever wanted, and I had a few, as many as I could stand before they got to be a nuisance, and I said good riddance to bad rubbish, every one."

You came from garbage. You'll never amount to a hill of beans.

"And you know what? They told me the boy had gone to a better place. So I wondered if he went and died. And I thought, well. Best for him, isn't it? I need to have my tea now. I drink it by the bucket, camomile for arthritis. I look too young to have arthritis, don't I?"

"This is a very cheerful colour," he replied helplessly. The house was painted gleaming lemon enamel throughout.

"The welfare did it. Mr. Miller told them to use the best paint. He always looked after things very well."

It had obviously been done years ago. The walls were spattered and streaked with resinous lines, a gluey brown corona above the stove. There were turds everywhere and a dozen tin plates, some with remnants of cat food.

Ruby had told Gavin, "Mrs. Miller has good days and bad days. Don't expect too much."

He had never expected too much.

Gavin had a silly wish as he left Gwen's house. He wished that instead of Ruby waiting for him in that car outside, it could be his brother. *My fairy godbrother.* He laughed to himself.

She hadn't asked him anything about his life, would never know about her six grandchildren, would never meet Louise.

"She can't feel much for anything outside of herself except the cats," said Ruby.

"Her husband?"

"Left over twenty years ago."

"I don't think I'll be seeing her again. She said she thought she'd dreamt me. That's exactly how I've always thought of her."

"I did warn you. I'm sorry, but I should say this. Between you and me, she told me once she had this baby and how beautiful he was with his wise face. Said she was robbed one time, came home, and you were gone."

"Sounds like she had a pretty hard time."

"It was her illness. She loses track of things in a big way—likely couldn't remember you were there half the time."

Gavin started to laugh very hard. Ruby didn't seem to mind. She drove, looking straight ahead.

It was almost midnight when Gavin arrived home. The house was quiet: the twins asleep, Morgan downstairs playing a video game, Gale and Celia out. Louise sat with Dion, giving him a bottle. She said nothing but handed him the baby.

Dion watched his father's face grow toward him. He loved having him big and close and warm. Gavin held Dion up so he could look at him. His son, who would never have survived someone like Gwen. Dion studied his father and struggled to keep his head steady. Gavin's face was behaving oddly. Bits of it moved around, twitching, and water rippled from his eyes. Dion broke into huge smiles.

IT WAS LATE SEPTEMBER, just past midnight, so they had woolly socks and thick sweaters. The countryside around them sparked with small movements of combines and trucks, the lights from four little towns—and in the east sat a glow on the horizon where they had left the city behind.

But the sky was huge and black and perfect for the two of them, who had brought cocoa in a thermos and lawn chairs.

Gavin held the binoculars out to Morgan. Even without magnification, she could see so much in the sky it made her dizzy. "I feel like I'm falling."

"It's like that," said her dad. "I distinctly remember the first time I truly noticed the stars. I was on my way across the bridge with streetlights blazing and traffic roaring by, but for some reason, I had an urge to look up. And I stopped, right in the middle of the sidewalk, by myself, and I wondered how it was I'd never seen those millions of stars. And the longer I stared, the more stars appeared, until it was like I was looking down instead of up and was sinking deeper into them. And I got dizzy, like you. That's why I decided to figure out what some of them were named, because people used to have that information; they used to respect those kinds of things. And, of course, the gods were always changing people into stars for one reason or another, sometimes to save them from danger or sometimes as a reward. It was a kind of immortality."

"Didn't everyone think you were nuts?"

"For liking stars?"

"For standing in the middle of the sidewalk staring up."

"It was a Saturday night in the late sixties—it was quite usual. And pay attention. There are clusters you should recognize, although we can see more stars in them today than they could when the clusters were named. I like these because they are groups of sisters—the seven Pleiades, named for doves because they were turned into doves before they were set in the sky, and then their five half-sisters, the raunchy ones, are the Hyades. Sailors believed the Hyades sent rains and rough weather, but if the Hyades didn't come there would be no crop that year. They were useful bad girls. And guess what was the name of their little brother? Dion. Dionysus."

"I can picture the Bump as a star."

"Me, too."

They poured hot chocolate, leaned into their chairs, and sipped. Machines flickered mutely in distant fields. They looked upward for a while in silence. No bird sounds or crickets. The air was still and cool.

"Satellite," Morgan whispered.

Almost a star, but its dance was fast and efficient.

Gavin saw Morgan was shivering, so went quietly to the car for a sleeping bag. He folded it around her, chair and all.

"Dad?"

"Yeah."

"Did you ever see a UFO?"

"Nope. Wanted to, but was never blessed."

"You wanted to? Wouldn't you be freaked?"

"Don't know. Never saw one."

"You're a pretty nice dad."

"Thanks. You're a pretty nice kid. Now, point to Draco."

Morgan is in her house by the sea. She has to get upstairs, but the elevators don't work properly, and she knows they are dangerous. She climbs step after step, the walls curved and narrowing with each flight. Sometimes, she passes by a little wooden door, painted bright white, with a small knob. There is illumination from somewhere above, soft light, but the narrow staircase is suffocating. She does not want to be trapped and keeps ascending, ascending. The stairs end at a wall that has one cupboard door up high, hinged at the bottom, the knob at the top centre. She turns the knob, and the door swings down. She pulls herself up and crawls out.

At first, she sees nothing. There is no floor, no roof. Only clouds, white and fluffy. This worries her. She looks again, and there is a floor. She steps onto it.

She hears a sweet hum from wires in the city far below, feels the faint rush of a breeze in her ears. It is so easy. She has no apron, no skirt for the birds to grasp with their hundreds of beaks, but she knows those had only been dream birds and this is the real thing.

She runs for the edge without fear and launches herself into a familiar landscape with such speed, such joy she could die of it. *I knew it. I knew I could fly.*

Her parents sat curled together on the old couch downstairs, wakeful in a house of six dreamers, talking quietly with Roland.

When Gavin told Louise, she hadn't been surprised. She already knew Gwen. For years, she'd understood, more than Gavin had, who his mother might be. Whenever he spoke of this woman, unsure of his memories, she felt the touch of a wind carrying a pall of weakness, a cruelty that Gavin seemed oblivious to. And there had been a wistfulness as he searched and a triumph when he found Gwen that scared Louise.

"Tell the girls the truth," she said. "Not right away, if you can't, but soon."

"I don't want them to hate her."

"How could they hate your mother? She gave them you. And somehow, you came away . . ." Louise knew that something of Rachael in her resisted those things most in need of a voice. *He came away from that woman strong and smart and funny and caring.* ". . . a gifted person."

It was close enough. From the look he gave her, she knew he could ravish her on the spot.

Roland broke in. "Makes him sound like Cinderella, Louise. I don't think so. More like the Simpleton. A Fool on a Quest."

"What's all this, Roland? What've you been feeding your devious brain?"

"Stanley. I've been talking to Stanley—you know, that slobby PhD Rebecca left me for."

"You left her."

"She left me in spirit first. He's not so bad, pompous as hell, but he's a good pool player. But how Rebecca could think he'd be a fun guy, I'll never know—it'd be like having sex with Santa Claus. Anyway, I tell Stanley about your nightmares, and he sits in his fat chair with his fat gut, sucking away on his Meerschaum pipe, which is almost gagging me, and says, 'Hmm, reminds me of the sleeping beauty motifs, the sleeping princesses.' I go, 'Right, I see what you mean.' Like I know what in hell he's talking about. So he goes on about fairy tales and deep sleeps. The idea is that it's not necessarily a bad thing to die temporarily or get turned to stone; it happens all the time to adolescents or, you'll like this, Fools on a Quest, and something good comes out of it."

"After you die," said Gavin.

"Exactly. So maybe that knight was doing a favour trying to trap or kill you."

"I guess."

"And now you've vanquished the beast—no disrespect intended to your sainted mother—so the dreams will stop."

"You're wasting your life, genius."

"Nope. I was kissed by too many princesses—it's a trance."

"Half a wit's better than nothing, Roland."

"I realize this. My relatives are living proof. Louise, how's the beer situation? And did I happen to mention the Fool always gets to marry the king's daughter?"

"It's late. I'm going to bed."

"The Simpleton's going out for a smoke. Anybody joining me?"

The three of them sat for a while under stars that raged in the cold September sky.

"Oh, sick, there's a moth in here, and it looks exactly like a potato chip."

"I think it's pretty, Celia," Louise told her. "Look at the poor thing. Its feet are caught in the dishcloth."

"It's disgusting. I hate moths—they're too furry."

"Look at it. It imitates a dried leaf and those big eyes—how can you hate something so elegant?"

"You are very weird, Mother Louise; you are also too sentimental."

"I don't like to see things suffer. I am not in the least sentimental. Take the cloth and shake it outside."

"I'm not going near that thing. Just stick it in the garbage."

"I'll put it out myself. Don't you have a date tonight?"

"A date? Mom, I don't think people actually have dates anymore. Saddle shoes and dopey seventies clothes might have come back for a while, but not dates, thank God. But, yes, I am going somewhere with a person of the male persuasion, and I will try not to get too pregnant."

"Really, Celia."

"You know, you are starting to sound a whole lot like Gramma."

"I am not."

"Well, you sound different; you say things you never used to."

"I do not. Like what?"

"Like, you always ask if I'm all right."

"Well, are you?"

"See, there you go. Why do you keep saying that?"

"I don't. Or maybe I asked and you didn't notice until now."

"No. I think you worry more."

"Maybe, but it's my job."

"Cut it out. It bugs me. I'm fine. Always was and always

will be. That should cover all answers for my lifetime, all right? And if I'm not, there's nothing you can do about it. If you read more women's magazines, you would know that."

"Besides, Celia, I never wore saddle shoes; that was before my time." *Damn.* She has said it finally: *my time.*

"Don't get all worked up. Mom, I know you didn't have saddle shoes, and you want me to be happy, and I am going to a movie with Ryan and then for a drive or a walk or something, and I won't compromise my virtue, and I'll take the moth out."

"I'm not upset. And thanks for telling me about Ryan. And thanks for the moth. And have fun."

"Listen."

"What. What's the matter?"

"No. *Shh.* Listen."

Then Louise could hear it. A low, throaty laugh, unfamiliar, coming from somewhere.

They found Gale sitting cross-legged on the living room floor. Her face, inches from Dion's, was as radiant as Joan of Arc's. Gale understood the moment and was oblivious to the others; everything was the Bump. She pulled her face back and put it up close to him, and he waited for a second, blank, as something struggled, then welled and broke the surface, and his arms flew up, and he burst. They heard it, his belly laugh, like the bells of an armistice, rich and wonderful to their ears.

Louise wrote on the calendar. September 25. *Dion Laughed.*

The End

About Harriet Richards

Harriet Richards was born in Toronto, Ontario, as the fifth of seven children to a Welsh father and an American mother. Her family relocated to the prairies during her childhood. Initially pursuing a career as a visual artist, her creative focus shifted when an obstinate painting, inspired by a recurring dream, evolved into her first short story.

Richards is the author of three acclaimed works of fiction. *The Lavender Child* (1998) was a finalist for the Fiction Award and won the First Book Award at the Saskatchewan Book Awards. *Waiting for the Piano Tuner to Die* (2003) was a finalist for Book of the Year, and *The Pious Robber* (2013) was also a finalist for Book of the Year and won the Fiction Award. Her short fiction has appeared in literary journals in Canada and Wales, and her paintings have been featured on book covers in both countries.

Richards has guided emerging writers through the Saskatchewan Writers' Guild and edited numerous works of fiction and literary essays for authors across Canada. She resides in Saskatoon, Saskatchewan.

About Shadowpaw Press

Shadowpaw Press is a traditional publishing company, located in Regina, Saskatchewan, Canada and founded in 2018 by Edward Willett, an award-winning author of science fiction, fantasy, and non-fiction for readers of all ages. A member of Literary Press Group (Canada) and the Association of Canadian Publishers, Shadowpaw Press publishes an eclectic selection of books by both new and established authors, including adult fiction, young adult fiction, children's books, non-fiction, and anthologies, plus new editions of notable, previously published books in any genre under the Shadowpaw Press Reprise imprint.

Email: publisher@shadowpawpress.com.

 facebook.com/shadowpawpress

 x.com/shadowpawpress

 instagram.com/shadowpawpress

Also from Shadowpaw Press

Literary Fiction

Hello by David Carpenter

Theories of Everything by Dwayne Brenna

Waiting for the Piano Tuner to Die by Harriet Richards

Let us be True by Erna Buffie

Dollybird by Anne Lazurko

Small Reckonings by Karin Melberg Schwier

Thickwood by Gayle M. Smith

Poetry

The Door at the End of Everything by Lynda Monahan

The Glass Lodge: 20th Anniversary Edition by John Brady McDonald

Phases by Belinda Betker

Stay by Katherine Lawrence

Nonfiction

The Crow Who Tampered With Time by Lloyd Ratzlaff

Backwater Mystic Blues by Lloyd Ratzlaff

Cupboard Love: A Dictionary of Culinary Curiosities by Mark Morton

www.ingramcontent.com/pod-product-compliance
Lightning Source LLC
Chambersburg PA
CBHW061529310726
48972CB00008B/2383